Tales From
Two Hemispheres

Hjalmar Hjorth Boysen

Contents

TALES FROM
TWO HEMISPHERES

BY

Hjalmar Hjorth Boysen

THE MAN WHO LOST HIS NAME.

ON the second day of June, 186--, a young Norseman, Halfdan Bjerk by name, landed on the pier at Castle Garden. He passed through the straight and narrow gate where he was asked his name, birthplace, and how much money he had,--at which he grew very much frightened.

"And your destination?"--demanded the gruff-looking functionary at the desk.

"America," said the youth, and touched his hat politely.

"Do you think I have time for joking?" roared the official, with an oath.

The Norseman ran his hand through his hair, smiled his timidly conciliatory smile, and tried his best to look brave; but his hand trembled and his heart thumped away at an alarmingly quickened tempo.

"Put him down for Nebraska!" cried a stout red-cheeked individual (inwrapped in the mingled fumes of tobacco and whisky) whose function it was to open and shut the gate.

"There ain't many as go to Nebraska."

"All right, Nebraska."

The gate swung open and the pressure from behind urged the timid traveler on, while an extra push from the gate-keeper sent him flying in the direction of a board fence, where he sat down and tried to realize that he was now in the land of liberty.

Halfdan Bjerk was a tall, slender-limbed youth of very delicate frame; he had a pair of wonderfully candid, unreflecting blue eyes, a smooth, clear, beardless face, and soft, wavy light hair, which was pushed back from his forehead without parting. His mouth and chin were well cut, but their lines were, perhaps, rather weak for a man. When in repose, the ensemble of his features was exceedingly pleasing and somehow reminded one of Correggio's St. John. He had left his native land because he was an ardent republican and was abstractly convinced that man, generically and individually, lives more happily in a republic than in a monarchy. He had anticipated with keen pleasure the large, freely breathing life he was to lead in a land where every man was his neighbor's brother, where no senseless traditions kept a jealous watch over obsolete systems and shrines, and no chilling prejudice blighted the spontaneous blossoming of the soul.

Halfdan was an only child. His father, a poor government official, had died during his infancy, and his mother had given music lessons, and kept boarders, in order to gain the means to give her son what is called a learned education. In the Latin school Halfdan had enjoyed the reputation of being a bright youth, and at the age of eighteen, he had entered the university under the most promising auspices. He could make very fair verses, and play all imaginable instruments with equal ease, which made him a favorite in society. Moreover, he possessed that very old-fashioned accomplishment of cutting silhouettes; and what was more, he could draw the most charmingly fantastic arabesques for embroidery patterns, and he even dabbled in portrait and landscape painting. Whatever he turned his hand to, he did well, in fact, astonishingly well for a dilettante, and yet not well enough to claim the title of an artist. Nor did it ever occur to him to make such a claim. As one of his fellow-students remarked in a fit of jealousy, "Once when Nature had made three geniuses, a poet, a musician, and a painter, she took all the remaining odds and ends and shook them together at random and the result was Halfdan Bjerk." This agreeable melange of accomplishments, however, proved very attractive to the ladies, who invited the possessor to innumerable afternoon tea-parties, where they drew heavy drafts on his unflagging patience, and kept him steadily engaged with patterns and designs for embroidery, leather flowers, and other dainty knick-knacks. And in return for all his exertions they called him "sweet" and "beautiful," and applied to him many other enthusiastic adjectives seldom heard in connection with masculine names. In the university, talents of this order gained but slight recognition, and when Halfdan had for three years been preparing himself in vain for the examen philosophicum, he found himself slowly and imperceptibly drifting into the ranks of the so-called studiosi perpetui, who preserve a solemn silence at the examination tables, fraternize with every new generation of freshmen, and at last become part of the fixed furniture of their Alma Mater. In the larger American colleges, such men are mercilessly dropped or sent to a Divinity School; but the

European universities, whose tempers the centuries have mellowed, harbor in their spacious Gothic bosoms a tenderer heart for their unfortunate sons. There the professors greet them at the green tables with a good-humored smile of recognition; they are treated with gentle forbearance, and are allowed to linger on, until they die or become tutors in the families of remote clergymen, where they invariably fall in love with the handsomest daughter, and thus lounge into a modest prosperity.

If this had been the fate of our friend Bjerk, we should have dismissed him here with a confident "vale" on his life's pilgrimage. But, unfortunately, Bjerk was inclined to hold the government in some way responsible for his own poor success as a student, and this, in connection with an aesthetic enthusiasm for ancient Greece, gradually convinced him that the republic was the only form of government under which men of his tastes and temperament were apt to flourish. It was, like everything that pertained to him, a cheerful, genial conviction, without the slightest tinge of bitterness. The old institutions were obsolete, rotten to the core, he said, and needed a radical renovation. He could sit for hours of an evening in the Students' Union, and discourse over a glass of mild toddy, on the benefits of universal suffrage and trial by jury, while the picturesqueness of his language, his genial sarcasms, or occasional witty allusions would call forth uproarious applause from throngs of admiring freshmen. These were the sunny days in Halfdan's career, days long to be remembered. They came to an abrupt end when old Mrs. Bjerk died, leaving nothing behind her but her furniture and some trifling debts. The son, who was not an eminently practical man, underwent long hours of misery in trying to settle up her affairs, and finally in a moment of extreme dejection sold his entire inheritance in a lump to a pawnbroker (reserving for himself a few rings and trinkets) for the modest sum of 250 dollars specie. He then took formal leave of the Students' Union in a brilliant speech, in which he traced the parallelisms between the lives of Pericles and Washington,--in his opinion the two greatest men the world had ever seen,--expounded his theory of democratic government, and explained the causes of the rapid rise of the American Republic. The next morning he exchanged half of his worldly possessions for a ticket to New York, and within a few days set sail for the land of promise, in the far West.

II.

From Castle Garden, Halfdan made his way up through Greenwich street, pursued by a clamorous troop of confidence men and hotel runners.

"Kommen Sie mit mir. Ich bin auch Deutsch," cried one. "Voila, voila, je parle Francais," shouted another, seizing hold of his valise. "Jeg er Dansk. Tale Dansk," [1] roared a third, with an accent which seriously impeached his truthfulness. In order to escape from these importunate rascals, who were every moment getting bolder, he threw himself into the first street-car which happened to pass; he sat down, gazed out of the windows and soon became so thoroughly absorbed in the animated scenes which moved as in a panorama before his eyes, that he quite forgot where he was going. The conductor called for fares, and received an English shilling, which, after some ineffectual expostulation, he pocketed, but gave no change. At last after about an hour's journey, the car stopped, the conductor called out "Central Park," and Halfdan woke up with a start. He dismounted with a timid, deliberate step, stared in dim bewilderment at the long rows of palatial residences, and a chill sense of loneliness crept over him. The hopeless strangeness of everything he saw, instead of filling him with rapture as he had once anticipated, Sent a cold shiver to his heart. It is a very large affair, this world of ours--a good deal larger than it appeared to him gazing out upon it from his snug little corner up under the Pole; and it was as unsympathetic as it was large; he suddenly felt what he had never been aware of before--that he was a very small part of it and of very little account after all. He staggered over to a bench at the entrance to the park, and sat long watching the fine carriages as they dashed past him; he saw the handsome women in brilliant costumes laughing and chatting gayly; the apathetic policemen promenading in stoic dignity up and down upon the smooth pavements; the jauntily attired nurses, whom in his Norse innocence he took for mothers or aunts of the children, wheeling baby-carriages which to Norse eyes seemed miracles of dainty ingenuity, under the shady crowns of the elm-trees. He did not know how long he had been sitting there, when a little bright-eyed girl with light kid gloves, a small blue parasol and a blue polonaise, quite a lady of fashion en miniature, stopped in front of him and stared at him in shy wonder. He had always been fond of children, and often rejoiced in their affectionate ways and confidential prattle, and now it suddenly touched him with a warm sense of human fellowship to have this little daintily befrilled and crisply starched beauty single him out for notice among the hundreds who reclined in the arbors, or sauntered to and fro under the great trees.

"What is your name, my little girl?" he asked, in a tone of friendly interest.

"Clara," answered the child, hesitatingly; then, having by another look assured herself of his harmlessness, she added: "How very funny you speak!"

"Yes," he said, stooping down to take he tiny begloved hand. "I do not speak as well as you do, yet; but I shall soon learn."

Clara looked puzzled.

"How old are you?" she asked, raising her parasol, and throwing back her head with an air of superiority.

"I am twenty-four years old."

She began to count half aloud on her fingers: "One, two, three, four," but, before she reached twenty, she lost her patience.

"Twenty-four," she exclaimed, "that is a great deal. I am only seven, and papa gave me a pony on my birthday. Have you got a pony?"

"No; I have nothing but what is in this valise, and you know I could not very well get a pony into it."

Clara glanced curiously at the valise and laughed; then suddenly she grew serious again, put her hand into her pocket and seemed to be searching eagerly for something. Presently she hauled out a small porcelain doll's head, then a red-painted block with letters on it, and at last a penny.

"Do you want them?" she said, reaching him her treasures in both hands. "You may have them all."

Before he had time to answer, a shrill, penetrating voice cried out:

"Why, gracious! child, what are you doing?"

And the nurse, who had been deeply absorbed in "The New York Ledger," came rushing up, snatched the child away, and retreated as hastily as she had come.

Halfdan rose and wandered for hours aimlessly along the intertwining roads and footpaths. He visited the menageries, admired the statues, took a very light dinner, consisting of coffee, sandwiches, and ice, at the Chinese Pavilion, and, toward evening, discovered an inviting leafy arbor, where he could withdraw into the privacy of his own thoughts, and ponder upon the still unsolved problem of his destiny. The little incident with the child had taken the edge off his unhappiness and turned him into a more conciliatory mood toward himself and the great pitiless world, which seemed to take so little notice of him. And he, who had come here with so warm a heart and so ardent a will to join in the great work of human advancement--to find himself thus harshly ignored and buffeted about, as if he were a hostile intruder! Before him lay the huge unknown city where human life pulsated with large, full heart-throbs, where a breathless, weird intensity, a cold, fierce passion seemed to be hurrying everything onward in a maddening whirl, where a gentle, warm-blooded enthusiast like himself had no place and could expect naught but a speedy destruction. A strange, unconquerable dread took possession of him, as if he had been caught in a swift, strong whirlpool, from which he vainly struggled to escape. He crouched down among the foliage and shuddered. He could not return to the city. No, no: he never would return. He would remain here hidden and unseen until morning, and then he would seek a vessel bound for his dear native land, where the great mountains loomed up in serene majesty toward the blue sky, where the pine-forests whispered their dreamily sympathetic legends, in the long summer twilights, where human existence flowed on in calm beauty with the modest aims, small virtues, and small vices which were the happiness of modest, idyllic souls. He even saw himself in spirit recounting to his astonished countrymen the wonderful things he had heard and seen during his foreign pilgrimage, and smiled to himself as he imagined their wonder when he should tell them about the beautiful little girl who had been the first and only one to offer him a friendly greeting in the strange land. During these reflections he fell asleep, and slept soundly for two or three hours. Once, he seemed to hear footsteps and whispers among the trees, and made an effort to rouse himself, but weariness again overmastered him and he slept on. At last, he felt himself seized violently by the shoulders, and a gruff voice shouted in his ear:

"Get up, you sleepy dog."

He rubbed his eyes, and, by the dim light of the moon, saw a Herculean policeman lifting a stout stick over his head. His former terror came upon him with increased violence, and his heart stood for a moment still, then, again, hammered away as if it would burst his sides.

"Come along!" roared the policeman, shaking him vehemently by the collar of his coat.

In his bewilderment he quite forgot where he was, and, in hurried Norse sentences, assured his persecutor that he was a harmless, honest traveler, and implored him to release him. But the official Hercules was inexorable.

"My valise, my valise;" cried Halfdan. "Pray let me get my valise."

They returned to the place where he had slept, but the valise was nowhere to be found. Then, with dumb despair he resigned himself to his fate, and after a brief ride on a street-car, found himself standing in a large, low-ceiled room; he covered his face with his hands and burst into tears.

"The grand-the happy republic," he murmured, "spontaneous blossoming of the soul. Alas! I have rooted up my life; I fear it will never blossom."

All the high-flown adjectives he had employed in his parting speech in the Students' Union, when he paid his enthusiastic tribute to the Grand Republic, now kept recurring to him, and in this moment the paradox seemed cruel. The Grand Republic, what did it care for such as he? A pair of brawny arms fit to wield the pick-axe and to steer the plow it received with an eager welcome; for a child-like, loving heart and a generously fantastic brain, it had but the stern greeting of the law.

III.

The next morning, Halfdan was released from the Police Station, having first been fined five dollars for vagrancy. All his money, with the exception of a few pounds which he had exchanged in Liverpool, he had lost with his valise, and he had to his knowledge not a single acquaintance in the city or on the whole continent. In order to increase his capital he bought some fifty "Tribunes," but, as it was already late in the day, he hardly succeeded in selling a single copy. The next morning, he once more stationed himself on the corner of Murray street and Broadway, hoping in his innocence to dispose of the papers he had still on hand from the previous day, and actually did find a few customers among the people who were jumping in and out of the omnibuses that passed up and down the great thoroughfare. To his surprise, however, one of these gentlemen returned to him with a very wrathful countenance, shook his fist at him, and vociferated with excited gestures something which to Halfdan's ears had a very unintelligible sound. He made a vain effort to defend himself; the situation appeared so utterly incomprehensible to him, and in his dumb helplessness he looked pitiful enough to move the heart of a stone. No English phrase suggested itself to him, only a few Norse interjections rose to his lips. The man's anger suddenly abated; he picked up the paper which he had thrown on the sidewalk, and stood for a while regarding Halfdan curiously.

"Are you a Norwegian?" he asked.

"Yes, I came from Norway yesterday."

"What's your name?"

"Halfdan Bjerk."

"Halfdan Bjerk! My stars! Who would have thought of meeting you here! You do not recognize me, I suppose."

Halfdan declared with a timid tremor in his voice that he could not at the moment recall his features.

"No, I imagine I must have changed a good deal since you saw me," said the man, suddenly dropping into Norwegian. "I am Gustav Olson, I used to live in the same house with you once, but that is long ago now."

Gustav Olson--to be sure, he was the porter's son in the house, where his mother had once during his childhood, taken a flat. He well remembered having clandestinely traded jack-knives and buttons with him, in spite of the frequent warnings he had received to have nothing to do with him; for Gustav, with his broad freckled face and red hair, was looked upon by the genteel inhabitants of the upper flats as rather a disreputable character. He had once whipped the son of a colonel who had been impudent to him, and thrown a snow-ball at the head of a new-fledged lieutenant, which offenses he had duly expiated at a house of correction. Since that time he had vanished from Halfdan's horizon. He had still the same broad freckled face, now covered with a lusty growth of coarse red beard, the same rebellious head of hair, which refused to yield to the subduing influences of the comb, the same plebeian hands and feet, and uncouth clumsiness of form. But his linen was irreproachable, and a certain dash in his manner, and the loud fashionableness of his attire, gave unmistakable evidences of prosperity.

"Come, Bjerk," said he in a tone of good-fellowship, which was not without its sting to the idealistic republican, "you must take up a better business than selling yesterday's `Tribune.' That won't pay here, you know. Come along to our office and I will see if something can't be done for you."

"But I should be sorry to give you trouble," stammered Halfdan, whose native pride, even in his present wretchedness, protested against accepting a favor from one whom he had been wont to regard as his inferior.

"Nonsense, my boy. Hurry up, I haven't much time to spare. The office is only two blocks from here. You don't look as if you could afford to throw away a friendly offer."

The last words suddenly roused Halfdan from his apathy; for he felt that they were true. A drowning man cannot afford to make nice distinctions--cannot afford to ask whether the helping hand that is extended to him be that of an equal or an inferior. So he swallowed his humiliation and threaded his way through the bewildering turmoil of Broadway, by the side of his officious friend.

They entered a large, elegantly furnished office, where clerks with sleek and severely apathetic countenances stood scribbling at their desks.

"You will have to amuse yourself as best you can," said Olson. "Mr. Van Kirk will be here in twenty minutes. I haven't time to entertain you."

A dreary half hour passed. Then the door opened and a tall, handsome man, with a full grayish beard, and a commanding presence, entered and took his seat at a desk in a smaller adjoining office. He opened, with great dispatch, a pile of letters which lay on the desk before him, called out in a sharp, ringing tone for a clerk, who promptly appeared, handed him half-a-dozen letters, accompanying each with a brief direction, took some clean paper from a drawer and fell to writing. There was something brisk, determined, and business-like in his manner, which made it seem very hopeless to Halfdan to appear before him as a petitioner. Presently Olson entered the private office, closing the door behind him, and a few minutes later reappeared and summoned Halfdan into the chief's presence.

"You are a Norwegian, I hear," said the merchant, looking around over his shoulder at the supplicant, with a preoccupied air. "You want work. What can you do?"

What can you do? A fatal question. But here was clearly no opportunity for mental debate. So, summoning all his courage, but feeling nevertheless very faint, he answered:

"I have passed both examen artium and philosophicum, [2] and got my laud clear in the former, but in the latter haud on the first point."

Mr. Van Kirk wheeled round on his chair and faced the speaker:

"That is all Greek to me," he said, in a severe tone. "Can you keep accounts?"

"No. I am afraid not."

Keeping accounts was not deemed a classical accomplishment in Norway. It was only "trade-rats" who troubled themselves about such gross things, and if our Norseman had not been too absorbed with the problem of his destiny, he would have been justly indignant at having such a question put to him.

"Then you don't know book-keeping?"

"I think not. I never tried it."

"Then you may be sure you don't know it. But you must certainly have tried your hand at something. Is there nothing you can think of which might help you to get a living?"

"I can play the piano--and--and the violin."

"Very well, then. You may come this afternoon to my house. Mr. Olson will tell you the address. I will give you a note to Mrs. Van Kirk. Perhaps she will engage you as a music teacher for the children. Good morning."

IV.

At half-past four o'clock in the afternoon, Halfdan found himself standing in a large, dimly lighted drawing-room, whose brilliant upholstery, luxurious carpets, and fantastically twisted furniture dazzled and bewildered his senses. All was so strange, so strange; nowhere a familiar object to give rest to the wearied eye. Wherever he looked he saw his shabbily attired figure repeated in the long crystal mirrors, and he became uncomfortably conscious of his threadbare coat, his uncouth boots, and the general incongruity of his appearance. With every moment his uneasiness grew; and he was vaguely considering the propriety of a precipitate flight, when the rustle of a dress at the farther end of the room startled him, and a small, plump lady, of a daintily exquisite form, swept up toward him, gave a slight inclination of her head, and sank down into an easy-chair:

"You are Mr. ----, the Norwegian, who wishes to give music lessons?" she said, holding a pair of gold-framed eyeglasses up to her eyes, and running over the note which she held in her hand. It read as follows:

DEAR MARTHA,--The bearer of this note is a young Norwegian, I forgot to ascertain his name, a friend of Olson's. He wishes to teach music. If you can help the poor devil and give him something to do, you will oblige,

Yours,

H. V. K.

Mrs. Van Kirk was evidently, by at least twelve years, her husband's junior, and apparently not very far advanced in the forties. Her blonde hair, which was freshly crimped, fell lightly over her smooth, narrow forehead; her nose, mouth and chin had a neat distinctness of outline; her complexion was either naturally or artificially perfect, and her eyes, which were of the purest blue, had, owing to their near-sightedness, a certain pinched and scrutinizing look. This look, which was without the slightest touch of severity, indicating merely a lively degree of interest, was further emphasized by three small perpendicular wrinkles, which deepened and again relaxed according to the varying intensity of observation she bestowed upon the object which for the time engaged her attention.

"Your name, if you please?" said Mrs. Van Kirk, having for awhile measured her visitor with a glance of mild scrutiny.

"Halfdan Bjerk."

"Half-dan B----, how do you spell that?"

"B-j-e-r-k."

"B-jerk. Well, but I mean, what is your name in English?"

Halfdan looked blank, and blushed to his ears.

"I wish to know," continued the lady energetically, evidently anxious to help him out, "what your name would mean in plain English. Bjerk, it certainly must mean something."

"Bjerk is a tree--a birch-tree."

"Very well, Birch,--that is a very respectable name. And your first name? What did you say that was?

"H-a-l-f-d-a-n."

"Half Dan. Why not a whole Dan and be done with it? Dan Birch, or rather Daniel Birch. Indeed, that sounds quite Christian."

"As you please, madam," faltered the victim, looking very unhappy.

"You will pardon my straightforwardness, won't you? B-jerk. I could never pronounce that, you know."

"Whatever may be agreeable to you, madam, will be sure to please me."

"That is very well said. And you will find that it always pays to try to please me. And you wish to teach music? If you have no objection I will call my oldest daughter. She is an excellent judge of music, and if your playing meets with her approval, I will engage you, as my husband suggests, not to teach Edith, you understand, but my youngest child, Clara."

Halfdan bowed assent, and Mrs. Van Kirk rustled out into the hall where she rang a bell, and re-entered. A servant in dress-coat appeared, and again vanished as noiselessly as he had come. To our Norseman there was some thing weird and uncanny about these silent entrances and exits; he could hardly suppress a shudder. He had been accustomed to hear the clatter of people's heels upon the bare floors, as they approached, and the audible crescendo of their footsteps gave one warning, and prevented one from being taken by surprise. While absorbed in these reflections, his senses must have been dormant; for just then Miss Edith Van Kirk entered, unheralded by anything but a hovering perfume, the effect of which was to lull him still deeper into his wondering abstraction.

"Mr. Birch," said Mrs. Van Kirk, "this is my daughter Miss Edith," and as Halfdan sprang to his feet and bowed with visible embarrassment, she continued:

"Edith, this is Mr. Daniel Birch, whom your father has sent here to know if he would be serviceable as a music teacher for Clara. And now, dear, you will have to decide about the merits of Mr. Birch. I don't know enough about music to be anything of a judge."

"If Mr. Birch will be kind enough to play," said Miss Edith with a languidly musical intonation," I shall be happy to listen to him."

Halfdan silently signified his willingness and followed the ladies to a smaller apartment which was separated from the drawing-room by folding doors. The apparition of the beautiful young girl who was walking at his side had suddenly filled him with a strange burning and shuddering happiness; he could not tear his eyes away from her; she held him as by a powerful spell. And still, all the while he had a painful sub-consciousness of his own unfortunate appearance, which was thrown into cruel relief by her splendor. The tall, lithe magnificence of her form, the airy elegance of her toilet, which seemed the perfection of self-concealing art, the elastic deliberateness of her step--all wrought like a gentle, deliciously soothing opiate upon the Norseman's fancy and lifted him into hitherto unknown regions of mingled misery and bliss. She seemed a combination of the most divine contradictions, one moment supremely conscious, and in the next adorably child-like and simple, now full of arts and coquettish innuendoes, then again naive, unthinking and almost boyishly blunt and direct; in a word, one of those miraculous New York girls whom abstractly one may disapprove of, but in the concrete must abjectly adore. This easy predominance of the masculine heart over the masculine reason in the presence of an impressive woman, has been the motif of a thousand tragedies in times past, and will inspire a thousand more in times to come.

Halfdan sat down at the grand piano and played Chopin's Nocturne in G major, flinging out that elaborate filigree of sound with an impetuosity and superb ABANDON which caused the ladies to exchange astonished glances behind his back. The transitions from the light and ethereal texture of melody to the simple, more concrete theme, which he rendered with delicate shadings of articulation, were sufficiently startling to impress even a less cultivated ear than that of Edith Van Kirk, who had, indeed, exhausted whatever musical resources New York has to offer. And she was most profoundly impressed. As he glided over the last pianissimo notes toward the two concluding chords (an ending so characteristic of Chopin) she rose and hurried to his side with a heedless eagerness, which was more eloquent than emphatic words of praise.

"Won't you please repeat this passage?" she said, humming the air with soft modulations; "I have always regarded the monotonous repetition of this strain" (and she indicated it lightly by a few touches of the keys) "as rather a blemish of an otherwise perfect composition. But as you play it, it is anything but monotonous. You put into this single phrase a more intense meaning and a greater variety of thought than I ever suspected it was capable of expressing."

"It is my favorite composition," answered he, modestly. "I have bestowed more thought upon it than upon anything I have ever played, unless perhaps it be the one in G minor, which, with all its difference of mood and phraseology, expresses an essentially kindred thought."

"My dear Mr. Birch," exclaimed Mrs. Van Kirk, whom his skillful employment of technical terms (in spite of his indifferent accent) had impressed even more than his rendering of the music,--"you are a comsummate{sic} artist, and we shall deem it a great privilege if you will undertake to instruct our child. I have listened to you with profound satisfaction."

Halfdan acknowledged the compliment by a bow and a blush, and repeated the latter part of the nocturne according to Edith's request.

"And now," resumed Edith, "may I trouble you to play the G minor, which has even puzzled me more than the one you have just played."

"It ought really to have been played first," replied Halfdan. "It is far intenser in its coloring and has a more passionate ring, but its conclusion does not seem to be final. There is no rest in it, and it seems oddly enough to be a mere transition into the major, which is its proper supplement and completes the fragmentary thought."

Mother and daughter once more telegraphed wondering looks at each other, while Halfdan plunged into the impetuous movements of the minor nocturne, which he played to the end with ever-increasing fervor and animation.

"Mr. Birch," said Edith, as he arose from the piano with a flushed face, and the agitation of the music still tingling through his nerves. "You are a far greater musician than you seem to be aware of. I have not been taking lessons for some time, but you have aroused all my musical ambition, and if you will accept me too, as a pupil, I shall deem it a favor."

"I hardly know if I can teach you anything," answered he, while his eyes dwelt with keen delight on her beautiful form. "But in my present position I can hardly afford to decline so flattering an offer."

"You mean to say that you would decline it if you were in a position to do so," said she, smiling.

"No, only that I should question my convenience more closely."

"Ah, never mind. I take all the responsibility. I shall cheerfully consent to being imposed upon by you."

Mrs. Van Kirk in the mean while had been examining the contents of a fragrant Russia-leather pocket-book, and she now drew out two crisp ten-dollar notes, and held them out toward him.

"I prefer to make sure of you by paying you in advance," said she, with a cheerfully familiar nod, and a critical glance at his attire, the meaning of which he did not fail to detect. "Somebody else might make the same discovery that we have made to-day, and outbid us. And we do not want to be cheated out of our good fortune in having been the first to secure so valuable a prize."

"You need have no fear on that score, madam," retorted Halfdan, with a vivid blush, and purposely misinterpreting the polite subterfuge. "You may rely upon my promise. I shall be here again, as soon as you wish me to return."

"Then, if you please, we shall look for you to-morrow morning at ten o'clock."

And Mrs. Van Kirk hesitatingly folded up her notes and replaced them in her pocket-book.

To our idealist there was something extremely odious in this sudden offer of money. It was the first time any one had offered to pay him, and it seemed to put him on a level with a common day-laborer. His first impulse was to resent it as a gratuitous humiliation, but a glance at Mrs. Van Kirk's countenance, which was all aglow with officious benevolence, re-assured him, and his indignation died away.

That same afternoon Olson, having been informed of his friend's good fortune, volunteered a loan of a hundred dollars, and accompanied him to a fashionable tailor, where he underwent a pleasing metamorphosis.

V.

In Norway the ladies dress with the innocent purpose of protecting themselves against the weather; if this purpose is still remotely present in the toilets of American women of to-day, it is, at all events, sufficiently disguised to challenge detection, very much like a primitive Sanscrit root in its French and English derivatives. This was the reflection which was uppermost in Halfdan's mind as Edith, ravishing to behold in the airy grace of her fragrant morning toilet, at the appointed time took her seat at his side before the piano. Her presence seemed so intense, so all-absorbing, that it left no thought for the music. A woman, with all the spiritual mysteries which that name implies, had always appeared to him rather a composite phenomenon, even apart from those varied accessories of dress, in which as by an inevitable analogy, she sees fit to express the inner multiformity of her being. Nevertheless, this former conception of his, when compared to that wonderful complexity of ethereal lines, colors, tints and half-tints which go to make up the modern New York girl, seemed inexpressibly simple, almost what plain arithmetic must appear to a man who has mastered calculus.

Edith had opened one of those small red-covered volumes of Chopin where the rich, wondrous melodies lie peacefully folded up like strange exotic flowers in an herbarium. She began to play the fantasia impromtu, which ought to be dashed off at a single "heat," whose passionate impulse hurries it on breathlessly toward its abrupt finale. But Edith toiled considerably with her fingering, and blurred the keen edges of each swift phrase by her indistinct articulation. And still there was a sufficiently ardent intention in her play to save it from being a failure. She made a gesture of disgust when she had finished, shut the book, and let her hands drop crosswise in her lap.

"I only wanted to give you a proof of my incapacity," she said, turning her large luminous gaze upon her instructor, "in order to make you duly appreciate what you have undertaken. Now, tell me truly and honestly, are you not discouraged?"

"Not by any means," replied he, while the rapture of her presence rippled through his nerves, "you have fire enough in you to make an admirable musician. But your fingers, as yet, refuse to carry out your fine intentions. They only need discipline."

"And do you suppose you can discipline them? They are a fearfully obstinate set, and cause me infinite mortification."

"Would you allow me to look at your hand?"

She raised her right hand, and with a sort of impulsive heedlessness let it drop into his. An exclamation of surprise escaped him.

"If you will pardon me," he said, "it is a superb hand--a hand capable of performing miracles--musical miracles I mean. Only look here"--(and he drew the fore and second fingers apart)--"so firmly set in the joint and still so flexible. I doubt if Liszt himself can boast a finer row of fingers. Your hands will surely not prevent you from becoming a second Von Bulow, which to my mind means a good deal more than a second Liszt."

"Thank you, that is quite enough," she exclaimed, with an incredulous laugh; "you have done bravely. That at all events throws the whole burden of responsibility upon myself, if I do not become a second somebody. I shall be perfectly satisfied, however, if you can only make me as good a musician as you are yourself, so that I can render a not too difficult piece without feeling all the while that I am committing sacrilege in mutilating the fine thoughts of some great composer."

"You are too modest; you do not--"

"No, no, I am not modest," she interrupted him with an impetuosity which startled him. "I beg of you not to persist in paying me compliments. I get too much of that cheap article elsewhere. I hate to be told that I am better than I know I am. If you are to do me any good by your instruction, you must be perfectly sincere toward me, and tell me plainly of my short-comings. I promise you beforehand that I shall never be offended. There is my hand. Now, is it a bargain?"

His fingers closed involuntarily over the soft beautiful hand, and once more the luxury of her touch sent a thrill of delight through him.

"I have not been insincere," he murmured, "but I shall be on my guard in future, even against the appearance of insincerity."

"And when I play detestably, you will say so, and not smooth it over with unmeaning flatteries?"

"I will try."

"Very well, then we shall get on well together. Do not imagine that this is a mere feminine whim of mine. I never was more in earnest. Men, and I believe foreigners, to a greater degree than Americans, have the idea that women must be treated with gentle forbearance; that their follies, if they are foolish, must be glossed over with some polite name. They exert themselves to the utmost to make us mere playthings, and, as such, contemptible both in our own eyes and in theirs. No sincere respect can exist where the truth has to be avoided. But the majority of American women are made of too stern a stuff to be dealt with in that way. They feel the lurking insincerity even where politeness forbids them to show it, and it makes them disgusted both with themselves, and with the flatterer. And now you must pardon me for having spoken so plainly to you on so short an acquaintance; but you are a foreigner, and it may be an act of friendship to initiate you as soon as possible into our ways and customs."

He hardly knew what to answer. Her vehemence was so sudden, and the sentiments she had uttered so different from those which he had habitually ascribed to women, that he could only sit and gaze at her in mute astonishment. He could not but admit that in the main she had judged him rightly, and that his own attitude and that of other men toward her sex, were based upon an implied assumption of superiority.

"I am afraid I have shocked you," she resumed, noticing the startled expression of his countenance. "But really it was quite inevitable, if we were at all to understand each other. You will forgive me, won't you?"

"Forgive!" stammered he, "I have nothing to forgive. It was only your merciless truthfulness which startled me. I rather owe you thanks, if you will allow me to be grateful to you. It seems an enviable privilege."

"Now," interrupted Edith, raising her forefinger in playful threat, "remember your promise."

The lesson was now continued without further interruption. When it was finished, a little girl, with her hair done up in curl-papers, and a very stiffly starched dress, which stood out on all sides almost horizontally, entered, accompanied by Mrs. Van Kirk. Halfdan immediately recognized his acquaintance from the park, and it appeared to him a good omen that this child, whose friendly interest in him had warmed his heart in a moment when his fortunes seemed so desperate, should continue to be associated with his life on this new continent. Clara was evidently greatly impressed by the change in his appearance, and could with difficulty be restrained from commenting upon it.

She proved a very apt scholar in music, and enjoyed the lessons the more for her cordial liking of her teacher.

It will be necessary henceforth to omit the less significant details in the career of our friend "Mr. Birch." Before a month was past, he had firmly established himself in the favor of the different members of the Van Kirk family. Mrs. Van Kirk spoke of him to her lady visitors as "a perfect jewel," frequently leaving them in doubt as to whether he was a cook or a coachman. Edith apostrophized him to her fashionable friends as "a real genius," leaving a dim impression upon their minds of flowing locks, a shiny velvet jacket, slouched hat, defiant neck-tie and a general air of disreputable pretentiousness. Geniuses of the foreign type were never, in the estimation of fashionable New York society, what you would call "exactly nice," and against prejudices of this order no amount of argument will ever prevail. Clara, who had by this time discovered that her teacher possessed an inexhaustible fund of fairy stories, assured her playmates across the street that he was "just splendid," and frequently invited them over to listen to his wonderful tales. Mr. Van Kirk himself, of course, was non-committal, but paid the bills unmurmuringly.

Halfdan in the meanwhile was vainly struggling against his growing passion for Edith; but the more he rebelled the more hopelessly he found himself entangled in its inextricable net. The fly, as long as it keeps quiet in the spider's web, may for a moment forget its situation; but the least effort to escape is apt to frustrate itself and again reveal the imminent peril. Thus he too "kicked against the pricks," hoped, feared, rebelled against his destiny, and again, from sheer weariness, relapsed into a dull, benumbed apathy. In spite of her friendly sympathy, he never felt so keenly his alienism as in her presence. She accepted the spontaneous homage he paid her, sometimes with impatience, as something that was really beneath her notice; at other times she frankly recognized it, bantered him with his "Old World chivalry," which would soon evaporate in the practical American atmosphere, and called him her Viking, her knight and her faithful squire. But it never occurred to her to regard his devotion in a serious light, and to look upon him as a possible lover had evidently never entered her head. As their intercourse grew more intimate, he had volunteered to read his favorite poets with her, and had gradually succeeded in imparting to her something of his own passionate liking for Heine and Bjoernson. She had in return called his attention to the works of American authors who had hitherto been little more than names to him, and they had thus managed to be of mutual benefit to each other, and to spend many a pleasant hour during the long winter afternoons in each other's company. But Edith had a very keen sense of humor, and could hardly restrain her secret amusement when she heard him reading Long-fellow's "Psalm of Life" and Poe's "Raven" (which had been familiar to her from her babyhood), often with false accent, but always with intense enthusiasm. The reflection that he had had no part of his life in common with her,--that he did not love the things which she loved,--could not share her prejudices (and women have a feeling akin to contempt for a man who does not respond to their prejudices)--

removed him at times almost beyond the reach of her sympathy. It was interesting enough as long as the experience was novel, to be thus unconsciously exploring another person's mind and finding so many strange objects there; but after a while the thing began to assume an uncomfortably serious aspect, and then there seemed to be something almost terrible about it. At such times a call from a gentleman of her own nation, even though he were one of the placidly stupid type, would be a positive relief; she could abandon herself to the secure sense of being at home; she need fear no surprises, and in the smooth shallows of their talk there were no unsuspected depths to excite and to baffle her ingenuity. And, again, reverting in her thought to Halfdan, his conversational brilliancy would almost repel her, as something odious and un-American, the cheap result of outlandish birth and unrepublican education. Not that she had ever valued republicanism very highly; she was one of those who associated politics with noisy vulgarity in speech and dress, and therefore thanked fortune that women were permitted to keep aloof from it. But in the presence of this alien she found herself growing patriotic; that much-discussed abstraction, which we call our country (and which is nothing but the aggregate of all the slow and invisible influences which go toward making up our own being), became by degrees a very palpable and intelligible fact to her.

Frequently while her American self was thus loudly asserting itself, Edith inflicted many a cruel wound upon her foreign adorer. Once,--it was the Fourth of July, more than a year after Halfdan's arrival, a number of young ladies and gentlemen, after having listened to a patriotic oration, were invited in to an informal luncheon. While waiting, they naturally enough spent their time in singing national songs, and Halfdan's clear tenor did good service in keeping the straggling voices together. When they had finished, Edith went up to him and was quite effusive in her expressions of gratitude.

"I am sure we ought all to be very grateful to you, Mr. Birch," she said, "and I, for my part, can assure you that I am."

"Grateful? Why?" demanded Halfdan, looking quite unhappy.

"For singing OUR national songs, of course. Now, won't you sing one of your own, please? We should all be so delighted to hear how a Swedish--or Norwegian, is it?--national song sounds."

"Yes, Mr. Birch, DO sing a Swedish song," echoed several voices.

They, of course, did not even remotely suspect their own cruelty. He had, in his enthusiasm for the day allowed himself to forget that he was not made of the same clay as they were, that he was an exile and a stranger, and must ever remain so, that he had no right to share their joy in the blessing of liberty. Edith had taken pains to dispel the happy illusion, and had sent him once more whirling toward his cold native Pole. His passion came near choking him, and, to conceal his impetuous emotion, he flung himself down on the piano-stool, and struck some introductory chords with perhaps a little superfluous emphasis. Suddenly his voice burst out into the Swedish national anthem, "Our Land, our Land, our Fatherland," and the air shook and palpitated with strong martial melody. His indignation, his love and his misery, imparted strength to his voice, and its occasional tremble in the PIANO passages was something more than an artistic intention. He was loudly applauded as he arose, and the young ladies thronged about him to ask if he "wouldn't please write out the music for them."

Thus month after month passed by, and every day brought its own misery. Mrs. Van Kirk's patronizing manners, and ostentatious kindness, often tested his patience to the utmost. If he was guilty of an innocent witticism or a little quaintness of expression, she always assumed it to be a mistake of terms and corrected him with an air of benign superiority. At times, of course, her corrections were legitimate, as for instance, when he spoke of WEARING a cane, instead of CARRYING one, but in nine cases out of ten the fault lay in her own lack of imagination and not in his ignorance of English. On such occasions Edith often took pity on him, defended him against her mother's criticism, and insisted that if this or that expression was not in common vogue, that was no reason why it should not be used, as it was perfectly grammatical, and, moreover, in keeping with the spirit of the language. And he, listening passively in admiring silence to her argument, thanked her even for the momentary pain because it was followed by so great a happiness. For it was so sweet to be defended by Edith, to feel that he and she were standing together side by side against the outer world. Could he only show her in the old heroic manner how much he loved her! Would only some one that was dear to her die, so that he, in that breaking down of social barriers which follows a great calamity, might comfort her in her sorrow. Would she then, perhaps, weeping, lean her wonderful head upon his breast, feeling but that he was a fellow-mortal, who had a heart that was loyal and true, and forgetting, for one brief instant, that he was a foreigner. Then, to touch that delicate Elizabethan frill which wound itself so daintily about Edith's neck--what inconceivable rapture! But it was quite impossible. It could never be. These were selfish thoughts, no doubt, but they were a lover's selfishness, and, as such, bore a close kinship to all that is purest and best in human nature.

It is one of the tragic facts of this life, that a relation so unequal as that which existed between Halfdan and Edith, is at all possible. As for Edith, I must admit that she was well aware that her teacher was in love with her. Women have wonderfully keen senses for phenomena of that kind, and it is an illusion if any one imagines, as our Norseman did, that he has locked his secret securely in the hidden chamber of his heart. In fleeting intonations, unconscious glances and attitudes, and through a hundred other channels it will make its way out, and the bereaved jailer may still clasp his key in fierce triumph, never knowing that he has been robbed. It was of course no fault of Edith's that she had become possessed of Halfdan's heart-secret. She regarded it as on the whole rather an absurd affair, and prized it very lightly. That a love so strong and yet so humble, so destitute of hope and still so unchanging, reverent and faithful, had something grand and touching in it, had never occurred to her. It is a truism to say that in our social code the value of a man's character is determined by his position; and fine traits in a foreigner (unless he should happen to be something very great) strike us rather as part of a supposed mental alienism, and as such, naturally suspicious. It is rather disgraceful than otherwise to have your music teacher in love with you, and critical friends will never quite banish the suspicion that you have encouraged him.

Edith had, in her first delight at the discovery of Halfdan's talent, frankly admitted him to a relation of apparent equality. He was a man of culture, had the manners and bearing of a gentleman, and had none of those theatrical airs which so often raise a sort of invisible wall between foreigners and Americans. Her mother, who loved to play the patron, especially to young men, had invited him to dinner-parties and introduced him to their friends, until almost every one looked upon him as a protege of the family. He appeared so well in a parlor, and had really such a distinguished presence, that it was a pleasure to look at him. He was remarkably free from those obnoxious traits which generalizing American travelers have led us to believe were inseparable from foreign birth; his finger-nails were in no way conspicuous; he did not, as a French count, a former adorer of Edith's, had done, indulge an unmasculine taste for diamond rings (possibly because he had none); his politeness was unobtrusive and subdued, and of his accent there was just enough left to give an agreeable color of individuality to his speech. But, for all that, Edith could never quite rid herself of the impression that he was intensely un-American. There was a certain idyllic quiescence about him, a child-like directness and simplicity, and a total absence of "push," which were startlingly at variance with the spirit of American life. An American could never have been content to remain in an inferior position without trying, in some way, to better his fortunes. But Halfdan could stand still and see, without the faintest stirring of envy, his plebeian friend Olson, whose education and talents could bear no comparison with his own, rise rapidly above him, and apparently have no desire to emulate him. He could sit on a cricket in a corner, with Clara on his lap, and two or three little girls nestling about him, and tell them fairy stories by the hour, while his kindly face beamed with innocent happiness. And if Clara, to coax him into continuing the entertainment, offered to kiss him, his measure of joy was full. This fair child, with her affectionate ways, and her confiding prattle, wound herself ever more closely about his homeless heart, and he clung to her with a touching devotion. For she was the only one who seemed to be unconscious of the difference of blood, who had not yet learned that she was an American and he--a foreigner.

VI.

Three years had passed by and still the situation was unchanged. Halfdan still taught music and told fairy stories to the children. He had a good many more pupils now than three years ago, although he had made no effort to solicit patronage, and had never tried to advertise his talent by what he regarded as vulgar and inartistic display. But Mrs. Van Kirk, who had by this time discovered his disinclination to assert himself, had been only the more active; had "talked him up" among her aristocratic friends; had given musical soirees, at which she had coaxed him to play the principal role, and had in various other ways exerted herself in his behalf. It was getting to be quite fashionable to admire his quiet, unostentatious style of playing, which was so far removed from the noisy bravado and clap-trap then commonly in vogue. Even professional musicians began to indorse him, and some, who had discovered that "there was money in him," made him tempting offers for a public engagement. But, with characteristic modesty, he distrusted their verdict; his sensitive nature shrank from anything which had the appearance of self-assertion or display.

But Edith--ah, if it had not been for Edith he might have found courage to enter at the door of fortune, which was now opened ajar. That fame, if he should gain it, would bring him any nearer to her, was a thought that was alien to so unworldly a temperament as his. And any action that had no bearing upon his relation to her, left him cold--seemed unworthy of the effort. If she had asked him to play in public; if she had required of him to go to the North Pole, or to cut his own throat, I verily believe he would have done it. And at last Edith did ask him to play. She and Olson had plotted together, and from the very friendliest motives agreed to play into each other's hands.

"If you only WOULD consent to play," said she, in her own persuasive way, one day as they had finished their lesson, "we should all be so happy. Only think how proud we should be of your success, for you know there is nothing you can't do in the way of music if you really want to."

"Do you really think so?" exclaimed he, while his eyes suddenly grew large and luminous.

"Indeed I do," said Edith, emphatically.

"And if--if I played well," faltered he, "would it really please you?"

"Of course it would," cried Edith, laughing; "how can you ask such a foolish question?"

"Because I hardly dared to believe it."

"Now listen to me," continued the girl, leaning forward in her chair, and beaming all over with kindly officiousness; "now for once you must be rational and do just what I tell you. I shall never like you again if you oppose me in this, for I have set my heart upon it; you must promise beforehand that you will be good and not make any objection. Do you hear?"

When Edith assumed this tone toward him, she might well have made him promise to perform miracles. She was too intent upon her benevolent scheme to heed the possible inferences which he might draw from her sudden display of interest.

"Then you promise?" repeated she, eagerly, as he hesitated to answer.

"Yes, I promise."

"Now, you must not be surprised; but mamma and I have made arrangements with Mr. S---- that you are to appear under his auspices at a concert which is to be given a week from to-night. All our friends are going, and we shall take up all the front seats, and I have already told my gentlemen friends to scatter through the audience, and if they care anything for my favor, they will have to applaud vigorously."

Halfdan reddened up to his temples, and began to twist his watch-chain nervously.

"You must have small confidence in my ability," he murmured, "since you resort to precautions like these."

"But my dear Mr. Birch," cried Edith, who was quick to discover that she had made a mistake, "it is not kind in you to mistrust me in that way. If a New York audience were as highly cultivated in music as you are, I admit that my precautions would be superfluous. But the papers, you know, will take their tone from the audience, and therefore we must make use of a little innocent artifice to make sure of it. Everything depends upon the success of your first public appearance, and if your friends can in this way help you to establish the reputation which is nothing but your right, I am sure you ought not to bind their hands by your foolish sensitiveness. You don't know the American way of doing things as well as I do, therefore you must stand by your promise, and leave everything to me."

It was impossible not to believe that anything Edith chose to do was above reproach. She looked so bewitching in her excited eagerness for his welfare that it would have been inhuman to oppose her. So he meekly succumbed, and began to discuss with her the programme for the concert.

During the next week there was hardly a day that he did not read some startling paragraph in the newspapers about "the celebrated Scandinavian pianist," whose appearance at S---- Hall was looked forward to as the principal event of the coming season. He inwardly rebelled against the well-meant exaggerations; but as he suspected that it was Edith's influence which was in this way asserting itself in his behalf, he set his conscience at rest and remained silent.

The evening of the concert came at last, and, as the papers stated the next morning, "the large hall was crowded to its utmost capacity with a select and highly appreciative audience." Edith must have played her part of the performance skillfully, for as he walked out upon the stage, he was welcomed with an enthusiastic burst of applause, as if he had been a world-renowned artist. At Edith's suggestion, her two favorite nocturnes had been placed first upon the programme; then followed one of those ballads of Chopin, whose rhythmic din and rush sweep onward, beleaguering the ear like eager, melodious hosts, charging in thickening ranks and columns, beating impetuous retreats, and again uniting with one grand emotion the wide-spreading army of sound for the final victory. Besides these, there was one of Liszt's "Rhapsodies Hongroises," an impromptu by Schubert, and several orchestral pieces; but the greater part of the programme was devoted to Chopin, because Halfdan, with his great, hopeless passion laboring in his breast, felt that he could interpret Chopin better than he could any other composer. He carried his audience by storm. As he retired to the dressing-room, after having finished the last piece, his friends, among whom Edith and Mrs. Van Kirk were the most conspicuous, thronged about him, showering their praises and congratulations upon him. They insisted with much friendly urging upon taking him home in their carriage; Clara kissed him, Mrs. Van Kirk introduced him to her lady acquaintances as "our friend, Mr. Birch," and Edith held his hand so long in hers that he came near losing his presence of mind and telling her then and there that he loved her. As his eyes rested on her, they became suddenly suffused with tears, and a vast bewildering happiness vibrated through his frame. At last he tore himself away and wandered aimlessly through the long, lonely streets. Why could he not tell Edith that he loved her? Was there any disgrace in loving? This heavenly passion which so suddenly had transfused his being, and year by year deadened the substance of his old self, creating in its stead something new and wild and strange which he never could know, but still held infinitely dear--had it been sent to him merely as a scourge to test his capacity for suffering?

Once, while he was a child, his mother had told him that somewhere in this wide world there lived a maiden whom God had created for him, and for him alone, and when he should see her, he should love her, and his life should thenceforth be all for her. It had hardly occurred to him, then, to question whether she would love him in return, it had appeared so very natural that she should. Now he had found this maiden, and she had been very kind to him; but her kindness had been little better than cruelty, because he had demanded something more than kindness. And still he had never told her of his love. He must tell her even this very night while the moon rode high in the heavens and all the small differences between human beings seemed lost in the vast starlit stillness. He knew well that by the relentless glare of the daylight his own insignificance would be cruelly conspicuous in the presence of her splendor; his scruples would revive, and his courage fade.

The night was clear and still. A clock struck eleven in some church tower near by. The Van Kirk mansion rose tall and stately in the moonlight, flinging a dense mass of shadow across the street. Up in the third story he saw two windows lighted; the curtains were drawn, but the blinds were not closed. All the rest of the house was dark. He raised his voice and sang a Swedish serenade which seemed in perfect concord with his own mood. His clear tenor rose through the silence of the night, and a feeble echo flung it back from the mansion opposite:

[3] "Star, sweet star, that brightly beamest,
Glittering on the skies nocturnal,
Hide thine eye no more from me,
Hide thine eye no more from me!"

The curtain was drawn aside, the window cautiously raised, and the outline of Edith's beautiful head appeared dark and distinct against the light within. She instantly recognized him.

"You must go away, Mr. Birch," came her voice in an anxious whisper out of the shadow. "Pray go away. You will wake up the people."

Her words were audible enough, but they failed to convey any meaning to his excited mind. Once more his voice floated upward to her opened window:

"And I yearn to reach thy dwelling,
Yearn to rise from earth's fierce turmoil;
Sweetest star upward to thee,

Yearn to rise, bright star to thee."

"Dear Mr. Birch," she whispered once more in tones of distress. "Pray DO go away. Or perhaps," she interrupted herself "--wait one moment and I will come down."

Presently the front door was noiselessly opened, and Edith's tall, lithe form, dressed in a white flowing dress, and with her blonde hair rolling loosely over her shoulders, appeared for an instant, and then again vanished. With one leap Halfdan sprang up the stairs and pushed through the half-opened door. Edith closed the door behind him, then with rapid steps led the way to the back parlor where the moon broke feebly through the bars of the closed shutters.

"Now Mr. Birch," she said, seating herself upon a lounge, "you may explain to me what this unaccountable behavior of yours means. I should hardly think I had deserved to be treated in this way by you."

Halfdan was utterly bewildered; a nervous fit of trembling ran through him, and he endeavored in vain to speak. He had been prepared for passionate reproaches, but this calm severity chilled him through, and he could only gasp and tremble, but could utter no word in his defense.

"I suppose you are aware," continued Edith, in the same imperturbable manner, "that if I had not interrupted you, the policeman would have heard you, and you would have been arrested for street disturbance. Then to-morrow we should have seen it in all the newspapers, and I should have been the laughing-stock of the whole town."

No, surely he had never thought of it in that light; the idea struck him as entirely new. There was a long pause. A cock crowed with a drowsy remoteness in some neighboring yard, and the little clock on the mantel-piece ticked on patiently in the moonlit dusk.

"If you have nothing to say," resumed Edith, while the stern indifference in her voice perceptibly relaxed, "then I will bid you good-night."

She arose, and with a grand sweep of her drapery, moved toward the door.

"Miss Edith," cried he, stretching his hands despairingly after her, "you must not leave me."

She paused, tossed her hair back with her hands, and gazed at him over her shoulder. He threw himself on his knees, seized the hem of her dress, and pressed it to his lips. It was a gesture of such inexpressible humility that even a stone would have relented.

"Do not be foolish, Mr. Birch," she said, trying to pull her dress away from him. "Get up, and if you have anything rational to say to me, I will stay and listen."

"Yes, yes," he whispered, hoarsely, "I shall be rational. Only do not leave me."

She again sank down wearily upon the lounge, and looked at him in expectant silence.

"Miss Edith," pleaded he in the same hoarse, passionate undertone, "have pity on me, and do not despise me. I love you--oh--if you would but allow me to die for you, I should be the happiest of men."

Again he shuddered, and stood long gazing at her with a mute, pitiful appeal. A tear stole into Edith's eye and trickled down over her cheek.

"Ah, Mr. Birch," she murmured, while a sigh shook her bosom, "I am sorry--very sorry that this misfortune has happened to you. You have deserved a better fate than to love me--to love a woman who can never give you anything in return for what you give her."

"Never?" he repeated mournfully, "never?"

"No, never! You have been a good friend to me, and as such I value you highly, and I had hoped that you would always remain so. But I see that it cannot be. It will perhaps be best for you henceforth not to see me, at least not until--pardon the expression--you have outlived this generous folly. And now, you know, you will need me no more. You have made a splendid reputation, and if you choose to avail yourself of it, your fortune is already made. I shall always rejoice to hear of your success, and--and if you should ever need a FRIEND, you must come to no one but me. I know that these are feeble words, Mr. Birch, and if they seem cold to you, you must pardon me. I can say nothing more."

They were indeed feeble words, although most cordially spoken. He tried to weigh them, to measure their meaning, but his mind was as if benumbed, and utterly incapable of thought. He walked across the floor, perhaps only to do something, not feeling where he trod, but still with an absurd sensation that he was taking immoderately long steps. Then he stopped abruptly, wrung his hands, and gazed at Edith. And suddenly, like a flash in a vacuum, the thought shot through his brain that he had seen this very scene somewhere--in a dream, in a remote childhood, in a previous existence, he did not know when or where. It seemed strangely familiar, and in the next instant strangely meaningless and unreal. The walls, the floor--everything began to move, to whirl about him; he struck his hands against his forehead, and sank down into a damask-covered easy-chair. With a faint cry of alarm, Edith sprang up, seized a bottle of cologne which happened to be within reach, and knelt down at his side. She put her arm around his neck, and raised his head.

"Mr. Birch, dear Mr. Birch," she cried, in a frightened whisper, "for God's sake come to yourself! O God, what have I done?"

She blew the eau-de-cologne into his face, and, as he languidly opened his eyes, he felt the touch of her warm hand upon his cheeks and his forehead.

"Thank heaven! he is better," she murmured, still continuing to bathe his temples. "How do you feel now, Mr. Birch?" she added, in a tone of anxious inquiry.

"Thank you, it was an unpardonable weakness," he muttered, without changing his attitude. "Do not trouble yourself about me. I shall soon be well."

It was so sweet to be conscious of her gentle ministry, that it required a great effort, an effort of conscience, to rouse him once more, as his strength returned.

"Had you not better stay?" she asked, as he rose to put on his overcoat. "I will call one of the servants and have him show you a room. We will say to-morrow morning that you were taken ill, and nobody will wonder."

"No, no," he responded, energetically. "I am perfectly strong now." But he still had to lean on a chair, and his face was deathly pale.

"Farewell, Miss Edith," he said; and a tender sadness trembled in his voice. "Farewell. We shall--probably--never meet again."

"Do not speak so," she answered, seizing his hand. "You will try to forget this, and you will still be great and happy. And when fortune shall again smile upon you, and--and--you will be content to be my friend, then we shall see each other as before."

"No, no," he broke forth, with a sudden hoarseness. "It will never be."

He walked toward the door with the motions of one who feels death in his limbs; then stopped once more and his eyes lingered with inexpressible sadness on the wonderful, beloved form which stood dimly outlined before him in the twilight. Then Edith's measure of misery, too, seemed full. With the divine heedlessness which belongs to her sex, she rushed up toward him, and remembering only that he was weak and unhappy, and that he suffered for her sake, she took his face between her hands and kissed him. He was too generous a man to misinterpret the act; so he whispered but once more: "Farewell," and hastened away.

VII.

After that eventful December night, America was no more what it had been to Halfdan Bjerk. A strange torpidity had come over him; every rising day gazed into his eyes with a fierce unmeaning glare. The noise of the street annoyed him and made him childishly fretful, and the solitude of his own room seemed still more dreary and depressing. He went mechanically through the daily routine of his duties as if the soul had been taken out of his work, and left his life all barrenness and desolation. He moved restlessly from place to place, roamed at all times of the day and night through the city and its suburbs, trying vainly to exhaust his physical strength; gradually, as his lethargy deepened into a numb, helpless despair, it seemed somehow to impart a certain toughness to his otherwise delicate frame. Olson, who was now a junior partner in the firm of Remsen, Van Kirk and Co., stood by him faithfully in these days of sorrow. He was never effusive in his sympathy, but was patiently forbearing with his friend's whims and moods, and humored him as if he had been a sick child intrusted to his custody. That Edith might be the moving cause of Olson's kindness was a thought which, strangely enough, had never occurred to Halfdan.

At last, when spring came, the vacancy of his mind was suddenly invaded with a strong desire to revisit his native land. He disclosed his plan to Olson, who, after due deliberation and several visits to the Van Kirk mansion, decided that the pleasure of seeing his old friends and the scenes of his childhood might push the painful memories out of sight, and renew his interest in life. So, one morning, while the May sun shone with a soft radiance upon the beautiful harbor, our Norseman found himself standing on the deck of a huge black-hulled Cunarder, shivering in spite of the warmth, and feeling a chill loneliness creeping over him at the sight of the kissing and affectionate leave-takings which were going on all around him. Olson was running back and forth, attending to his baggage; but he himself took no thought, and felt no more responsibility than if he had been a helpless child. He half regretted that his own wish had prevailed, and was inclined to hold his friend responsible for it; and still he had not energy enough to protest now when the journey seemed inevitable. His heart still clung to the place which held the corpse of his ruined life, as a man may cling to the spot which hides his beloved dead.

About two weeks later Halfdan landed in Norway. He was half reluctant to leave the steamer, and the land of his birth excited no emotion in his breast. He was but conscious of a dim regret that he was so far away from Edith. At last, however, he betook himself to a hotel, where he spent the afternoon sitting with half-closed eyes at a window, watching listlessly the drowsy slow-pulsed life which dribbled languidly through the narrow thoroughfare. The noisy uproar of Broadway chimed remotely in his ears, like the distant roar of a tempest-tossed sea, and what had once been a perpetual annoyance was now a sweet memory. How often with Edith at his side had he threaded his way through the surging crowds that pour, on a fine afternoon, in an unceasing current up and down the street between Union and Madison Squares. How friendly, and sweet, and gracious, Edith had been at such times; how fresh her voice, how witty and animated her chance remarks when they stopped to greet a passing acquaintance; and, above all, how inspiring the sight of her heavenly beauty. Now that was all past. Perhaps he should never see Edith again.

The next day he sauntered through the city, meeting some old friends, who all seemed changed and singularly uninteresting. They were all engaged or married, and could talk of nothing but matrimony, and their prospects of advancement in the Government service. One had an influential uncle who had been a chum of the present minister of finance; another based his hopes of future prosperity upon the family connections of his betrothed, and a third was waiting with a patient perseverance, worthy of a better cause, for the death or resignation of an antiquated chef-de-bureau, which, according to the promise of some mighty man, would open a position for him in the Department of Justice. All had the most absurd theories about American democracy, and indulged freely in prophecies of coming disasters; but about their own government they had no opinion whatever. If Halfdan attempted to set them right, they at once grew excited and declamatory; their opinions were based upon conviction and a charming ignorance of facts, and they were not to be moved. They knew all about Tweed and the Tammany Ring, and believed them to be representative citizens of New York, if not of the United States; but of Charles Sumner and Carl Schurz they had never heard. Halfdan, who, in spite of his misfortunes in the land of his adoption, cherished a very tender feeling for it, was often so thoroughly aroused at the foolish prejudices which everywhere met him, that his torpidity gradually thawed away, and he began to look more like his former self.

Toward autumn he received an invitation to visit a country clergyman in the North, a distant relative of his father's, and there whiled away his time, fishing and shooting, until winter came. But as Christmas drew near, and the day wrestled feebly with the all-conquering night, the old sorrow revived. In the darkness which now brooded over land and sea, the thoughts needed no longer be on guard against themselves; they could roam far and wide as they listed. Where was Edith now, the sweet, the wonderful Edith? Was there yet the same dancing light in her beautiful eyes, the same golden sheen in her hair, the same merry ring in her voice? And had she not said that when he was content to be only her friend, he might return to her, and she would receive him in the old joyous and confiding way? Surely there was no life to him apart from her: why should he not be her friend? Only a glimpse of her lovely face--ah, it was worth a lifetime; it would consecrate an age of misery, a glimpse of Edith's face. Thus ran his fancies day by day, and the night only lent a deeper intensity to the yearnings of the day. He walked about as in a dream, seeing nothing, heeding nothing, while this one strong desire--to see Edith once more--throbbed and throbbed with a slow, feverish perseverance within him. Edith--Edith, the very name had a strange, potent fascination. Every thought whispered "Edith,"--his pulse beat "Edith,"--and his heart repeated the beloved name. It was his pulse-beat,--his heartbeat,--his life-beat.

And one morning as he stood absently looking at his fingers against the light--and they seemed strangely wan and transparent--the thought at last took shape. It rushed upon him with such vehemence, that he could no more resist it. So he bade the clergyman good-bye, gathered his few worldly goods together and set out for Bergen. There he found an English steamer which carried him to Hull, and a few weeks later, he was once more in New York.

It was late one evening in January that a tug-boat arrived and took the cabin passengers ashore. The moon sailed tranquilly over the deep blue dome of the sky, the stars traced their glittering paths of light from the zenith downward, and it was sharp, bitter cold. Northward over the river lay a great bank of cloud, dense, gray and massive, the spectre of the coming snow-storm. There it lay so huge and fantastically human, ruffling itself up, as fowls do, in defense against the cold. Halfdan walked on at a brisk rate--strange to say, all the street-cars he met went the wrong way--startling every now and then some precious memory, some word or look or gesture of Edith's which had hovered long over those scenes, waiting for his recognition. There was the great jewel-store where Edith had taken him so often to consult his taste whenever a friend of hers was to be married. It was there that they had had an amicable quarrel over that bronze statue of Faust which she had found beautiful, while he, with a rudeness which seemed now quite incomprehensible, had insisted that it was not. And when he had failed to convince her, she had given him her hand in token of reconciliation--and Edith had a wonderful way of giving her hand, which made any one feel that it was a peculiar privilege to press it--and they had walked out arm in arm into the animated, gas-lighted streets, with a delicious sense of snugness and security, being all the more closely united for their quarrel. Here, farther up the avenue, they had once been to a party, and he had danced for the first time in his life with Edith. Here was Delmonico's, where they had had such fascinating luncheons together; where she had got a stain on her dress, and he had been forced to observe that her dress was then not really a part of herself, since it was a thing that could not be stained. Her dress had always seemed to him as something absolute and final, exalted above criticism, incapable of improvement.

As I have said, Halfdan walked briskly up the avenue, and it was something after eleven when he reached the house which he sought. The great cloud-bank in the north had then begun to expand and stretched its long misty arms eastward and westward over the heavens. The windows on the ground-floor were dark, but the sleeping apartments in the upper stories were lighted. In Edith's room the inside shutters were closed, but one of the windows was a little down at the top. And as he stood gazing with tremulous happiness up to that window, a stanza from Heine which he and Edith had often read together, came into his head. It was the story of the youth who goes to the Madonna at Kevlar and brings her as a votive offering a heart of wax, that she may heal him of his love and his sorrow.

"I bring this waxen image,
The image of my heart,
Heal thou my bitter sorrow,
And cure my deadly smart!" [4]

Then came the thought that for him, too, as for the poor youth of Cologne, there was healing only in death. And still in this moment he was so near Edith, should see her perhaps, and the joy at this was stronger than all else, stronger even than death. So he sat down beside the steps of the mansion opposite, where there was some shelter from the wind, and waited patiently till Edith should close her window. He was cold, perhaps, but, if so, he hardly knew it, for the near joy of seeing her throbbed warmly in his veins. Ah, there--the blinds were thrown open; Edith, in all the lithe magnificence of her wonderful form, stood out clear and beautiful against the light within; she pushed up the lower window in order to reach the upper one, and for a moment leaned out over the sill. Once more her wondrous profile traced itself in strong relief against the outer gloom. There came a cry from the street below, a feeble involuntary one, but still distinctly audible. Edith peered anxiously out into the darkness, but the darkness had grown denser and she could see nothing. The window was fastened, the shutters closed, and the broad pathway of light which she had flung out upon the night had vanished.

Halfdan closed his eyes trying to retain the happy vision. Yes, there she stood still, and there was a heavenly smile upon her lips--ugh, he shivered--the snow swept in a wild whirl up the street. He wrapped his plaid more closely about him, and strained his eyes to catch one more glimpse of the beloved Edith. Ah, yes; there she was again; she came nearer and nearer, and she touched his cheek, gently, warily smiling all the while with a strange wistful smile which was surely not Edith's. There, she bent over him,--touched him again,--how cold her hands were; the touch chilled him to the heart. The snow had now begun to fall in large scattered flakes, whirling fitfully through the air, following every chance gust of wind, but still falling, falling, and covering the earth with its white, death-like shroud.

But surely--there was Edith again,--how wonderful!--in a long snow-white robe, grave and gracious, still with the wistful smile on her lips. See, she beckons to him with her hand, and he rises to follow, but something heavy clings to his feet and he cannot stir from the spot. He tries to cry for help, but he cannot,--can only stretch out his hands to her, and feel very unhappy that he cannot follow her. But now she pauses in her flight, turns about, and he sees that she wears a myrtle garland in her hair like a bride. She comes toward him, her countenance all radiant with love and happiness, and she stoops down over him and speaks:

"Come; they are waiting for us. I will follow thee in life and in death, wherever thou goest. Come," repeats Edith, "they have long been waiting. They are all here."

And he imagines he knows who they all are, although he has never heard of them, nor can he recall their names.

"But--but," he stammers, "I--I--am a foreigner "

It appeared then that for some reason this was an insurmountable objection. And Edith's happiness dies out of her beautiful face, and she turns away weeping.

"Edith, beloved!"

Then she is once more at his side.

"Thou art no more a foreigner to me, beloved. Whatever thou art, I am."

And she presses her lips to his--it was the sweetest kiss of his life--the kiss of death.

The next morning, as Edith, after having put the last touch to her toilet, threw the shutters open, a great glare of sun-smitten snow burst upon her and for a moment blinded her eyes. On the sidewalk opposite, half a dozen men with snow-shovels in their hands and a couple of policeman had congregated, and, judging by their manner, were discussing some object of interest. Presently they were joined by her father, who had just finished his breakfast and was on his way to the office. Now he stooped down and gazed at something half concealed in the snow, then suddenly started back, and as she caught a glimpse of his face, she saw that it was ghastly white. A terrible foreboding seized her. She threw a shawl about her shoulders and rushed down-stairs. In the hall she was met by her father, who was just entering, followed by four men, carrying something between them. She well knew what it was. She would fain have turned away, but she could not: grasping her father's arm and pressing it hard, she gazed with blank, frightened eyes at the white face, the lines of which Death had so strangely emphasized. The snow-flakes which hung in his hair had touched him with their sudden age, as if to bridge the gulf between youth and death. And still he was beautiful--the clear brow, the peaceful, happy indolence, the frozen smile which death had perpetuated. Smiling, he had departed from the earth which had no place for him, and smiling entered the realm where, among the many mansions, there is, perhaps, also one for a gentle, simple-hearted enthusiast.

THE STORY OF AN OUTCAST.

THERE was an ancient feud between the families; and Bjarne Blakstad was not the man to make it up, neither was Hedin Ullern. So they looked askance at each other whenever they met on the highway, and the one took care not to cross the other's path. But on Sundays, when the church-bells called the parishioners together, they could not very well avoid seeing each other on the church-yard; and then, one day, many years ago, when the sermon had happened to touch Bjarne's heart, he had nodded to Hedin and said: "Fine weather to-day;" and Hedin had returned the nod and answered: "True is that." "Now I have done my duty before God and men," thought Bjarne, "and it is his turn to take the next step." "The fellow is proud," said Hedin to himself, "and he wants to show off his generosity. But I know the wolf by his skin, even if he has learned to bleat like a ewe-lamb."

What the feud really was about, they had both nearly forgotten. All they knew was that some thirty years ago there had been a quarrel between the pastor and the parish about the right of carrying arms to the church. And then Bjarne's father had been the spokesman of the parish, while Hedin's grandsire had been a staunch defender of the pastor. There was a rumor, too, that they had had a fierce encounter somewhere in the woods, and that the one had stabbed the other with a knife; but whether that was really true, no one could tell.

Bjarne was tall and grave, like the weather-beaten fir-trees in his mast-forest. He had a large clean-shaven face, narrow lips, and small fierce eyes. He seldom laughed, and when he did, his laugh seemed even fiercer than his frown. He wore his hair long, as his fathers had done, and dressed in the styles of two centuries ago; his breeches were clasped with large silver buckles at the knees, and his red jerkin was gathered about his waist with a leathern girdle. He loved everything that was old, in dress as well as in manners, took no newspapers, and regarded railroads and steamboats as inventions of the devil. Bjarne had married late in life, and his marriage had brought him two daughters, Brita and Grimhild.

Hedin Ullern was looked upon as an upstart. He could only count three generations back, and he hardly knew himself how his grandfather had earned the money that had enabled him to buy a farm and settle down in the valley. He had read a great deal, and was well informed on the politics of the day; his name had even been mentioned for storthingsmand, or member of parliament from the district, and it was the common opinion, that if Bjarne Blakstad had not so vigorously opposed him, he would have been elected, being the only "cultivated" peasant in the valley. Hedin was no unwelcome guest in the houses of gentlefolks, and he was often seen at the judge's and the pastor's omber parties. And for all this Bjarne Blakstad only hated him the more. Hedin's wife, Thorgerda, was fair-haired, tall and stout, and it was she who managed the farm, while her husband read his books, and studied politics in the newspapers; but she had a sharp tongue and her neighbors were afraid of her. They had one son, whose name was Halvard.

Brita Blakstad, Bjarne's eldest daughter, was a maid whom it was a joy to look upon. They called her "Glitter-Brita," because she was fond of rings and brooches, and everything that was bright; while she was still a child, she once took the old family bridal-crown out from the storehouse and carried it about on her head. "Beware of that crown, child," her father had said to her, "and wear it not before the time. There is not always blessing in the bridal silver." And she looked wonderingly up into his eyes and answered: "But it glitters, father;" and from that time forth they had named her Glitter-Brita.

And Glitter-Brita grew up to be a fair and winsome maiden, and wherever she went the wooers flocked on her path. Bjarne shook his head at her, and often had harsh words upon his lips, when he saw her braiding field-flowers into her yellow tresses or clasping the shining brooches to her bodice; but a look of hers or a smile would completely disarm him. She had a merry way of doing things which made it all seem like play; but work went rapidly from her hands, while her ringing laughter echoed through the house, and her sunny presence made it bright in the dusky ancestral halls. In her kitchen the long rows of copper pots and polished kettles shone upon the walls, and the neatly scoured milk-pails stood like soldiers on parade about the shelves under the ceiling. Bjarne would often sit for hours watching her, and a strange spring-feeling would steal into his heart. He felt a father's pride in her stately growth and her rich womanly beauty. "Ah!" he would say to himself, "she has the pure blood in her veins and, as true as I live, the farm shall be hers." And then, quite contrary to his habits, he would indulge in a little reverie, imagining the time when he, as an aged man, should have given the estate over into her hands, and seeing her as a worthy matron preside at the table, and himself rocking his grandchildren on his knee. No wonder, then, that he eyed closely the young lads who were beginning to hover about the house, and that he looked with suspicion upon those who selected Saturday nights for their visits. [5] When Brita was twenty years old, however, her father thought that it was time for her to make her choice. There were many fine, brave lads in the valley, and, as Bjarne thought, Brita would have the good sense to choose the finest and the bravest. So, when the winter came, he suddenly flung his doors open to the youth of the parish, and began to give parties with ale and mead in the grand old style. He even talked with the young men, at times, encouraged them to manly sports, and urged them to taste of his home-brewed drinks and to tread the spring-dance briskly. And Brita danced and laughed so that her hair flew around her and the silver brooches tinkled and rang on her bosom. But when the merriment was at an end, and any one of the lads remained behind to offer her his hand, she suddenly grew grave, told him she was too young, that she did not know herself, and that she had had no time as yet to decide so serious a question. Thus the winter passed and the summer drew near.

In the middle of June, Brita went to the saeter [6] with the cattle; and her sister, Grimhild, remained at home to keep house on the farm. She loved the life in the mountains; the great solitude sometimes made her feel sad, but it was not an unpleasant sadness, it was rather a gentle toning down of all the shrill and noisy feelings of the soul. Up there, in the heart of the primeval forest, her whole being seemed to herself a symphony of melodious whispers with a vague delicious sense of remoteness and mystery in them, which she only felt and did not attempt to explain. There, those weird legends which, in former days, still held their sway in the fancy of every Norsewoman, breathed their secrets into her ear, and she felt her nearness and kinship to nature, as at no other time.

One night, as the sun was low, and a purple bluish smoke hung like a thin veil over the tops of the forest, Brita had taken out her knitting and seated herself on a large moss-grown stone, on the croft. Her eyes wandered over the broad valley which was stretched out below, and she could see the red roofs of the Blakstad mansion peeping forth between the fir-trees. And she wondered what they were doing down there, whether Grimhild had done milking, and whether her father had returned from the ford, where it was his habit at this hour to ride with the footmen to water the horses. As she sat thus wondering, she was startled by a creaking in the dry branches hard by, and lifting her eye, she saw a tall, rather clumsily built, young man emerging from the thicket. He had a broad but low forehead, flaxen hair which hung down over a pair of dull ox-like eyes; his mouth was rather large and, as it was half open, displayed two massive rows of shining white teeth. His red peaked cap hung on the back of his head and, although it was summer, his thick wadmal vest was buttoned close up to his throat; over his right arm he had flung his jacket, and in his hand he held a bridle.

"Good evening," said Brita, "and thanks for last meeting;" although she was not sure that she had ever seen him before.

"It was that bay mare, you know," stammered the man in a half apologetic tone, and shook the bridle, as if in further explanation.

"Ah, you have lost your mare," said the girl, and she could not help smiling at his helplessness and his awkward manner.

"Yes, it was the bay mare," answered he, in the same diffident tone; then, encouraged by her smile, he straightened himself a little and continued rather more fluently: "She never was quite right since the time the wolves were after her. And then since they took the colt away from her the milk has been troubling her, and she hasn't been quite like herself."

"I haven't seen her anywhere hereabouts," said Brita; "you may have to wander far, before you get on the track of her."

"Yes, that is very likely. And I am tired already."

"Won't you sit down and rest yourself?"

He deliberately seated himself in the grass, and gradually gained courage to look her straight in the face; and his dull eye remained steadfastly fixed on her in a way which bespoke unfeigned surprise and admiration. Slowly his mouth broadened into a smile; but his smile had more of sadness than of joy in it. She had, from the moment she saw him, been possessed of a strangely patronizing feeling toward him. She could not but treat him as if he had been a girl or some person inferior to her in station. In spite of his large body, the impression he made upon her was that of weakness; but she liked the sincerity and kindness which expressed themselves in his sad smile and large, honest blue eyes. His gaze reminded her of that of an ox, but it had not only the ox's dullness, but also its simplicity and good-nature.

They sat talking on for a while about the weather, the cattle, and the prospects of the crops.

"What is your name?" she asked, at last.

"Halvard Hedinson Ullern."

A sudden shock ran through her at the sound of that name; in the next moment a deep blush stole over her countenance.

"And my name," she said, slowly, "is Brita Bjarne's daughter Blakstad."

She fixed her eyes upon him, as if to see what effect her words produced. But his features wore the same sad and placid expression; and no line in his face seemed to betray either surprise or ill-will. Then her sense of patronage grew into one of sympathy and pity. "He must either be weak-minded or very unhappy," thought she, "and what right have I then to treat him harshly." And she continued her simple, straightforward talk with the young man, until he, too, grew almost talkative, and the sadness of his smile began to give way to something which almost resembled happiness. She noticed the change and rejoiced. At last, when the sun had sunk behind the western mountain tops, she rose and bade him good-night; in another moment the door of the saeter-cottage closed behind her, and he heard her bolting it on the inside. But for a long time he remained sitting on the grass, and strange thoughts passed through his head. He had quite forgotten his bay mare.

The next evening when the milking was done, and the cattle were gathered within the saeter enclosure, Brita was again sitting on the large stone, looking out over the valley. She felt a kind of companionship with the people when she saw the smoke whirling up from their chimneys, and she could guess what they were going to have for supper. As she sat there, she again heard a creaking in the branches, and Halvard Ullern stood again before her, with his jacket on his arm, and the same bridle in his hand.

"You have not found your bay mare yet?" she exclaimed, laughingly. "And you think she is likely to be in this neighborhood?"

"I don't know," he answered; "and I don't care if she isn't."

He spread his jacket on the grass, and sat down on the spot where he had sat the night before. Brita looked at him in surprise and remained silent; she didn't know how to interpret this second visit.

"You are very handsome," he said, suddenly, with a gravity which left no doubt as to his sincerity.

"Do you think so?" she answered, with a merry laugh. He appeared to her almost a child, and it never entered her mind to feel offended. On the contrary, she was not sure but that she felt pleased.

"I have thought of you ever since yesterday," he continued, with the same imperturbable manner. "And if you were not angry with me, I thought I would like to look at you once more. You are so different from other folks."

"God bless your foolish talk," cried Brita, with a fresh burst of merriment. "No, indeed I am not angry with you; I should just as soon think of being angry with-- with that calf," she added for want of another comparison.

"You think I don't know much," he stammered. "And I don't." The sad smile again settled on his countenance.

A feeling of guilt sent the blood throbbing through her veins. She saw that she had done him injustice. He evidently possessed more sense, or at least a finer instinct, than she had given him credit for.

"Halvard," she faltered, "if I have offended you, I assure you I didn't mean to do it; and a thousand times I beg your pardon."

"You haven't offended me, Brita," answered he, blushing like a girl. "You are the first one who doesn't make me feel that I am not so wise as other folks."

She felt it her duty to be open and confiding with him in return; and in order not to seem ungenerous, or rather to put them on an equal footing by giving him also a peep into her heart, she told him about her daily work, about the merry parties at her father's house, and about the lusty lads who gathered in their halls to dance the Halling and the spring-dance. He listened attentively while she spoke, gazing earnestly into her face, but never interrupting her. In his turn he described to her in his slow deliberate way, how his father constantly scolded him because he was not bright, and did not care for politics and newspapers, and how his mother wounded him with her sharp tongue by making merry with him, even in the presence of the servants and strangers. He did not seem to imagine that there was anything wrong in what he said, or that he placed himself in a ludicrous light; nor did he seem to speak from any unmanly craving for sympathy. His manner was so simple and straightforward that what Brita probably would have found strange in another, she found perfectly natural in him.

It was nearly midnight when they parted{.} She hardly slept at all that night, and she was half vexed with herself for the interest she took in this simple youth. The next morning her father came up to pay her a visit and to see how the flocks were thriving. She understood that it would be dangerous to say anything to him about Halvard, for she knew his temper and feared the result, if he should ever discover her secret. Therefore, she shunned an opportunity to talk with him, and only busied herself the more with the cattle and the cooking. Bjarne soon noticed her distraction, but, of course, never suspected the cause. Before he left her, he asked her if she did not find it too lonely on the saeter, and if it would not be well if he sent her one of the maids for a companion. She hastened to assure him that that was quite unnecessary; the cattle-boy who was there to help her was all the company she wanted. Toward evening, Bjarne Blakstad loaded his horses with buckets, filled with cheese and butter, and started for the valley. Brita stood long looking after him as he descended the rocky slope, and she could hardly conceal from herself that she felt relieved, when, at last, the forest hid him from her sight. All day she had been walking about with a heavy heart; there seemed to be something weighing on her breast, and she could not throw it off. Who was this who had come between her and her father? Had she ever been afraid of him before, had she been glad to have him leave her? A sudden bitterness took possession of her, for in her distress, she gave Halvard the blame for all that had happened. She threw herself down on the grass and burst into a passionate fit of weeping; she was guilty, wretchedly miserable, and all for the sake of one whom she had hardly known for two days. If he should come in this moment, she would tell him what he had done toward her; and her wish must have been heard, for as she raised her eyes, he stood there at her side, the sad feature about his mouth and his great honest eyes gazing wonderingly at her. She felt her purpose melt within her; he looked so good and so unhappy. Then again came the thought of her father and of her own wrong, and the bitterness again revived.

"Go away," cried she, in a voice half reluctantly tender and half defiant. "Go away, I say; I don't want to see you any more."

"I will go to the end of the world if you wish it," he answered, with a strange firmness.

He picked up his jacket which he had dropped on the ground, then turned slowly, gave her mother long look, an infinitely sad and hopeless one, and went. Her bosom heaved violently--remorse, affection and filial duty wrestled desperately in her heart.

"No, no," she cried, "why do you go? I did not mean it so. I only wanted--"

He paused and returned as deliberately as he had gone.

Why should I dwell upon the days that followed--how her heart grew ever more restless, how she would suddenly wake up at nights and see those large blue eyes sadly gazing at her, how by turns she would condemn herself and him, and how she felt with bitter pain that she was growing away from those who had hitherto been nearest and dearest to her. And strange to say, this very isolation from her father made her cling only the more desperately to him. It seemed to her as if Bjarne had deliberately thrown her off; that she herself had been the one who took the first step had hardly occurred to her. Alas, her grief was as irrational as her love. By what strange devious process of reasoning these convictions became settled in her mind, it is difficult to tell. It is sufficient to know that she was a woman and that she loved. She even knew herself that she was irrational, and this very sense drew her more hopelessly into the maze of the labyrinth from which she saw no escape.

His visits were as regular as those of the sun. She knew that there was only a word of hers needed to banish him from her presence forever. And how many times did she not resolve to speak that word? But the word was never spoken. At times a company of the lads from the valley would come to spend a merry evening at the saeter; but she heeded them not, and they soon disappeared. Thus the summer went amid passing moods of joy and sorrow. She had long known that he loved her, and when at last his slow confession came, it added nothing to her happiness; it only increased her fears for the future. They laid many plans together in those days; but winter came as a surprise to both, the cattle were removed from the mountains, and they were again separated.

Bjarne Blakstad looked long and wistfully at his daughter that morning, when he came to bring her home. She wore no more rings and brooches, and it was this which excited Bjarne's suspicion that everything was not right with her. Formerly he was displeased because she wore too many; now he grumbled because she wore none.

II.

The winter was half gone; and in all this time Brita had hardly once seen Halvard. Yes, once,--it was Christmas-day,--she had ventured to peep over to his pew in the church, and had seen him, sitting at his father's side, and gazing vacantly out into the empty space; but as he had caught her glance, he had blushed, and began eagerly to turn the leaves of his hymn-book. It troubled her that he made no effort to see her; many an evening she had walked alone down at the river-side, hoping that he might come; but it was all in vain. She could not but believe that his father must have made some discovery, and that he was watched. In the mean time the black cloud thickened over her head; for a secret gnawed at the very roots of her heart. It was a time of terrible suspense and suffering--such as a man never knows, such as only a woman can endure. It was almost a relief when the cloud burst, and the storm broke loose, as presently it did.

One Sunday, early in April, Bjarne did not return at the usual hour from church. His daughters waited in vain for him with the dinner, and at last began to grow uneasy. It was not his habit to keep irregular hours. There was a great excitement in the valley just then; the America-fever had broken out. A large vessel was lying out in the fjord, ready to take the emigrants away; and there was hardly a family that did not mourn the loss of some brave-hearted son, or of some fair and cherished daughter. The old folks, of course, had to remain behind; and when the children were gone, what was there left for them but to lie down and die? America was to them as distant as if it were on another planet. The family feeling, too, has ever been strong in the Norseman's breast; he lives for his children, and seems to live his life over again in them. It is his greatest pride to be able to trace his blood back into the days of Sverre and St. Olaf, and with the same confidence he expects to see his race spread into the future in the same soil where once it has struck root. Then comes the storm from the Western seas, wrestles with the sturdy trunk, and breaks it; and the shattered branches fly to all the four corners of the heavens. No wonder, then, like a tree that has lost its crown, his strength is broken and he expects but to smoulder into the earth and die.

Bjarne Blakstad, like the sturdy old patriot that he was, had always fiercely denounced the America rage; and it was now the hope of his daughters that, perhaps, he had stayed behind to remind the restless ones among the youth of their duty toward their land, or to frighten some bold emigration agent who might have been too loud in his declamations. But it was already eight o'clock and Bjarne was not yet to be seen. The night was dark and stormy; a cold sleet fiercely lashed the window-panes, and the wind roared in the chimney. Grimhild, the younger sister, ran restlessly out and in and slammed the doors after her. Brita sat tightly pressed up against the wall in the darkest corner of the room. Every time the wind shook the house she started up; then again seated herself and shuddered. Dark forebodings filled her soul.

At last,--the clock had just struck ten,--there was a noise heard in the outer hall. Grimhild sprang to the door and tore it open. A tall, stooping figure entered, and by the dress she at once recognized her father.

"Good God," cried she, and ran up to him.

"Go away, child," muttered he, in a voice that sounded strangely unfamiliar, and he pushed her roughly away. For a moment he stood still, then stalked up to the table, and, with a heavy thump, dropped down into a chair. There he remained with his elbows resting on his knees, and absently staring on the floor. His long hair hung in wet tangles down over his face, and the wrinkles about his mouth seemed deeper and fiercer than usual. Now and then he sighed, or gave vent to a deep groan. In a while his eyes began to wander uneasily about the room; and as they reached the corner where Brita was sitting, he suddenly darted up, as if stung by something poisonous, seized a brand from the hearth, and rushed toward her.

"Tell me I did not see it," he broke forth, in a hoarse whisper, seizing her by the arm and thrusting the burning brand close up to her face. "Tell me it is a lie--a black, poisonous lie."

She raised her eyes slowly to his and gazed steadfastly into his face. "Ah," he continued in the same terrible voice, "it was what I told them down there at the church--a lie--an infernal lie. And I drew blood--blood, I say--I did--from the slanderer. Ha, ha, ha! What a lusty sprawl that was!"

The color came and departed from Brita's cheeks. And still she was strangely self possessed. She even wondered at her own calmness. Alas, she did not know that it was a calmness that is more terrible than pain, the corpse of a forlorn and hopeless heart.

"Child," continued Bjarne, and his voice assumed a more natural tone, "why dost thou not speak? They have lied about thee, child, because thou art fair, they have envied thee." Then, almost imploringly, "Open thy mouth, Brita, and tell thy father that thou art pure--pure as the snow, child--my own--my beautiful child."

There was a long and painful pause, in which the crackling of the brand, and the heavy breathing of the old man were the only sounds to break the silence. Pale like a marble image stood she before him; no word of excuse, no prayer for forgiveness escaped her; only a convulsive quivering of the lips betrayed the life that struggled within her. With every moment the hope died in Bjarne's bosom. His visage was fearful to behold. Terror and fierce indomitable hatred had grimly distorted his features, and his eyes burned like fire-coals beneath his bushy brows.

"Harlot," he shrieked, "harlot!"

A cold gust of wind swept through the room. The windows shook, the doors flew open, as if touched by a strong invisible hand--and the old man stood alone, holding the flickering brand above his head.

It was after midnight, the wind had abated, but the snow still fell, thick and silent, burying paths and fences under its cold white mantle. Onward she fled-- onward and ever onward. And whither, she knew not. A cold numbness had chilled her senses, but still her feet drove her irresistibly onward. A dark current seemed to have seized her, she only felt that she was adrift, and she cared not whither it bore her. In spite of the stifling dullness which oppressed her, her body seemed as light as air. At last,--she knew not where,--she heard the roar of the sea resounding in her ears, a genial warmth thawed the numbness of her senses, and she floated joyfully among the clouds--among golden, sun-bathed clouds. When she opened her eyes, she found herself lying in a comfortable bed, and a young woman with a kind motherly face was sitting at her side. It was all like a dream, and she made no effort to account for what appeared so strange and unaccountable.

What she afterward heard was that a fisherman had found her in a snow-drift on the strand, and that he had carried her home to his cottage and had given her over to the charge of his wife. This was the second day since her arrival. They knew who she was, but had kept the doors locked and had told no one that she was there. She heard the story of the good woman without emotion; it seemed an intolerable effort to think. But on the third day, when her child was born, her mind was suddenly aroused from its lethargy, and she calmly matured her plans; and for the child's sake she resolved to live and to act. That same evening there came a little boy with a bundle for her. She opened it and found therein the clothes she had left behind, and--her brooches. She knew that it was her sister who had sent them; then there was one who still thought of her with affection. And yet her first impulse was to send it all back, or to throw it into the ocean; but she looked at her child and forbore.

A week passed, and Brita recovered. Of Halvard she had heard nothing. One night, as she lay in a half doze, she thought she had Seen a pale, frightened face pressed up against the window-pane, and staring fixedly at her and her child; but, after all, it might have been merely a dream. For her fevered fancy had in these last days frequently beguiled her into similar visions. She often thought of him, but, strangely enough, no more with bitterness, but with pity. Had he been strong enough to be wicked, she could have hated him, but he was weak, and she pitied him. Then it was that; one evening, as she heard that the American vessel was to sail at daybreak, she took her little boy and wrapped him carefully in her own clothes, bade farewell to the good fisherman and his wife, and walked alone down to the strand. Huge clouds of fantastic shapes chased each other desperately along the horizon, and now and then the slender new moon glanced forth from the deep blue gulfs between. She chose a boat at random and was about to unmoor it, when she saw the figure of a man tread carefully over the stones and hesitatingly approach her.

"Brita," came in a whisper from the strand.

"Who's there?"

"It is I. Father knows it all, and he has nearly killed me; and mother, too."

"Is that what you have come to tell me?"

"No, I would like to help you some. I have been trying to see you these many days." And he stepped close up to the boat.

"Thank you; I need no help."

"But, Brita," implored he, "I have sold my gun and my dog, and everything I had, and this is what I have got for it." He stretched out his hand and reached her a red handkerchief with something heavy bound up in a corner. She took it mechanically, held it in her hand for a moment, then flung it far out into the water. A smile of profound contempt and pity passed over her countenance.

"Farewell, Halvard," said she, calmly, and pushed the boat into the water.

"But, Brita," cried he, in despair, "what would you have me do?"

She lifted the child in her arms, then pointed to the vacant seat at her side. He understood what she meant, and stood for a moment wavering. Suddenly, he covered his face with his hands and burst into tears. Within half an hour, Brita boarded the vessel, and as the first red stripe of the dawn illumined the horizon, the wind filled the sails, and the ship glided westward toward that land where there is a home for them whom love and misfortune have exiled.

It was a long and wearisome voyage. There was an old English clergyman on board, who collected curiosities; to him she sold her rings and brooches, and thereby obtained more than sufficient money to pay her passage. She hardly spoke to any one except her child. Those of her fellow-parishioners who knew her, and perhaps guessed her history, kept aloof from her, and she was grateful to them that they did. From morning till night, she sat in a corner between a pile of deck freight and the kitchen skylight, and gazed at her little boy who was lying in her lap. All her hopes, her future, and her life were in him. For herself, she had ceased to hope.

"I can give thee no fatherland, my child," she said to him. "Thou shalt never know the name of him who gave thee life. Thou and I, we shall struggle together, and, as true as there is a God above, who sees us, He will not leave either of us to perish. But let us ask no questions, child, about that which is past. Thou shalt grow and be strong, and thy mother must grow with thee."

During the third week of the voyage, the English clergyman baptized the boy, and she called him Thomas, after the day in the almanac on which he was born. He should never know that Norway had been his mother's home; therefore she would give him no name which might betray his race. One morning, early in the month of

June, they hailed land, and the great New World lay before them.

III.

Why should I speak of the ceaseless care, the suffering, and the hard toil, which made the first few months of Brita's life on this continent a mere continued struggle for existence? They are familiar to every emigrant who has come here with a brave heart and an empty purse. Suffice it to say that at the end of the second month, she succeeded in obtaining service as milkmaid with a family in the neighborhood of New York. With the linguistic talent peculiar to her people, she soon learned the English language and even spoke it well. From her countrymen, she kept as far away as possible, not for her own sake, but for that of her boy; for he was to grow great and strong, and the knowledge of his birth might shatter his strength and break his courage. For the same reason she also exchanged her picturesque Norse costume for that of the people among whom she was living. She went commonly by the name of Mrs. Brita, which pronounced in the English way, sounded very much like Mrs. Bright, and this at last became the name by which she was known in the neighborhood.

Thus five years passed; then there was a great rage for emigrating to the far West, and Brita, with many others, started for Chicago. There she arrived in the year 1852, and took up her lodgings with an Irish widow, who was living in a little cottage in what was then termed the outskirts of the city. Those who saw her in those days, going about the lumber-yards and doing a man's work, would hardly have recognized in her the merry Glitter-Brita, who in times of old trod the spring-dance so gayly in the well-lighted halls of the Blakstad mansion. And, indeed, she was sadly changed! Her features had become sharper, and the firm lines about her mouth expressed severity, almost sternness. Her clear blue eyes seemed to have grown larger, and their glance betrayed secret, ever-watchful care. Only her yellow hair had resisted the force of time and sorrow; for it still fell in rich and wavy folds over a smooth white forehead. She was, indeed, half ashamed of it, and often took pains to force it into a sober, matronly hood. Only at nights, when she sat alone talking with her boy, she would allow it to escape from its prison; and he would laugh and play with it, and in his child's way even wonder at the contrast between her stern face and her youthful maidenly tresses.

This Thomas, her son, was a strange child. He had a Norseman's taste for the fabulous and fantastic, and although he never heard a tale of Necken or the Hulder, he would often startle his mother by the most fanciful combinations of imagined events, and by bolder personifications than ever sprung from the legendary soil of the Norseland. She always took care to check him whenever he indulged in these imaginary flights, and he at last came to look upon them as something wrong and sinful. The boy, as he grew up, often strikingly reminded her of her father, as, indeed, he seemed to have inherited more from her own than from Halvard's race. Only the bright flaxen hair and his square, somewhat clumsy stature might have told him to be the latter's child. He had a hot temper, and often distressed his mother by his stubbornness; and then there would come a great burst of repentance afterwards, which distressed her still more. For she was afraid it might be a sign of weakness. "And strong he must be," said she to herself, "strong enough to overcome all resistance, and to conquer a great name for himself, strong enough to bless a mother who brought him into the world nameless."

Strange to say, much as she loved this child, she seldom caressed him. It was a penance she had imposed upon herself to atone for her guilt. Only at times, when she had been sitting up late, and her eyes would fall, as it were, by accident upon the little face on the pillow, with the sweet unconsciousness of sleep resting upon it like a soft, invisible veil, would she suddenly throw herself down over him, kiss him, and whisper tender names in his ear, while her tears fell hot and fast on his yellow hair and his rosy countenance. Then the child would dream that he was sailing aloft over shining forests, and that his mother, beaming with all the beauty of her lost youth, flew before him, showering golden flowers on his path. These were the happiest moments of Brita's joyless life, and even these were not unmixed with bitterness; for into the midst of her joy would steal a shy anxious thought which was the more terrible because it came so stealthily, so soft-footed and unbidden. Had not this child been given her as a punishment for her guilt? Had she then a right to turn God's scourge into a blessing? Did she give to God "that which belongeth unto God," as long as all her hopes, her thoughts, and her whole being revolved about this one earthly thing, her son, the child of her sorrow? She was not a nature to shrink from grave questions; no, she met them boldly, when once they were there, wrestled fiercely with them, was defeated, and again with a martyr's zeal rose to renew the combat. God had Himself sent her this perplexing doubt and it was her duty to bear His burden. Thus ran Brita's reasoning. In the mean while the years slipped by, and great changes were wrought in the world about her.

The few hundred dollars which Brita had been able to save, during the first three years of her stay in Chicago, she had invested in a piece of land. In the mean while the city had grown, and in the year 1859 she was offered five thousand dollars for her lot; this offer she accepted and again bought a small piece of property at a short distance from the city. The boy had since his eighth year attended the public school, and had made astonishing progress. Every day when school was out, she would meet him at the gate, take him by the hand and lead him home. If any of the other boys dared to make sport of her, or to tease him for his dependence upon her, it was sure to cost that boy a black eye{.} He soon succeeded in establishing himself in the respect of his school-mates, for he was the strongest boy of his own age, and ever ready to protect and defend the weak and defenseless. When Thomas Bright (for that was the name by which he was known) was fifteen years old he was offered a position as clerk in the office of a lumber-merchant, and with his mother's consent he accepted it. He was a fine young lad now, large and well-knit, and with a clear earnest countenance. In the evening he would bring home books to read, and as it had always been Brita's habit to interest herself in whatever interested him, she soon found herself studying and discussing with him things which had in former years been far beyond the horizon of her mind. She had at his request reluctantly given up her work in the lumber-yards, and now spent her days at home, busying herself with sewing and reading and such other things as women find to fill up a vacant hour.

One evening, when Thomas was in his nineteenth year, he returned from his office with a graver face than usual. His mother's quick eye immediately saw that something had agitated him, but she forbore to ask.

"Mother," said he at last, "who is my father? Is he dead or alive?"

"God is your father, my son," answered she, tremblingly. "If you love me, ask me no more."

"I do love you, mother," he said, and gave her a grave look, in which she thought she detected a mingling of tenderness and reproach. "And it shall be as you have said."

It was the first time she had had reason to blush before him, and her emotion came near overwhelming her; but with a violent effort she stifled it, and remained outwardly calm. He began pacing up and down the floor with his head bent and his hands on his back. It suddenly occurred to her that he was a grown man, and that she could no longer hold the same relation to him as his supporter and protector. "Alas," thought she, "if God will but let me remain his mother, I shall bless and thank Him."

It was the first time this subject had been broached, and it gave rise to many a doubt and many a question in the anxious mother's mind. Had she been right in concealing from him that which he might justly claim to know? What had been her motive in keeping him ignorant of his origin and of the land of his birth? She had wished him to grow to the strength of manhood, unconscious of guilt, so that he might bear his head upright, and look the world fearlessly in the face. And still, had there not in all this been a lurking thought of herself, a fear of losing his love, a desire to stand pure and perfect in his eye? She hardly dared to answer these questions, for, alas, she knew not that even our purest motives are but poorly able to bear a searching scrutiny. She began to suspect that her whole course with her son had been wrong from the very beginning. Why had she not told him the stern truth, even if he should despise her for it, even if she should have to stand a blushing culprit in his presence? Often, when she heard his footsteps in the hall, as he returned from the work of the day, she would man herself up and the words hovered upon her lips: "Son, thou art a bastard born, a child of guilt, and thy mother is an outcast upon the earth." But when she met those calm blue eyes of his, saw the unsuspecting frankness of his manner and the hopefulness with which he looked to the future, her womanly heart shrank from its duty, and she hastened out of the room, threw herself on her bed, and wept. Fiercely she wrestled with God in prayer, until she thought that even God had deserted her. Thus months passed and years, and the constant care and anxiety began to affect her health. She grew pale and nervous, and the slightest noise would annoy her. In the mean while, her manner toward the young man had become strangely altered, and he soon noticed it, although he forbore to speak. She was scrupulously mindful of his comfort, anxiously anticipated his wants, and observed toward him an ever vigilant consideration, as if he had been her master instead of her son.

When Thomas was twenty-two years of age, he was offered a partnership in his employer's business, and with every year his prospects brightened. The sale of his mother's property brought him a very handsome little fortune, which enabled him to build a fine and comfortable house in one of the best portions of the city. Thus their outward circumstances were greatly improved, and of comfort and luxury Brita had all and more than she had ever desired; but her health was broken down, and the physicians declared that a year of foreign travel and a continued residence in Italy might possibly restore her. At last, Thomas, too, began to urge her, until she finally yielded. It was on a bright morning in May that they both started for New York, and three days later they took the boat for Europe. What countries they were to visit they had hardly decided, but after a brief stay in England we find them again on a steamer bound for Norway.

IV.

Warm and gentle as it is, June often comes to the fjord-valleys of Norway with the voice and the strength of a giant. The glaciers totter and groan, as if in anger at their own weakness, and send huge avalanches of stones and ice down into the valleys. The rivers swell and rush with vociferous brawl out over the mountainsides, and a thousand tiny brooks join in the general clamor, and dance with noisy chatter over the moss-grown birch-roots. But later, when the struggle is at an end, and June has victoriously seated herself upon her throne, her voice becomes more richly subdued and brings rest and comfort to the ear and to the troubled heart. It was while the month was in this latter mood that Brita and her son entered once more the valley whence, twenty-five years ago, they had fled. Many strange, turbulent emotions stirred the mother's bosom, as she saw again the great snow-capped mountains, and the calm, green valley, her childhood's home, lying so snugly sheltered in their mighty embrace. Even Thomas's breast was moved with vaguely sympathetic throbs, as this wondrous scene spread itself before him. They soon succeeded in hiring a farm-house, about half an hour's walk from Blakstad, and, according to Brita's wish, established themselves there for the summer. She had known the people well, when she was young, but they never thought of identifying her with the merry maid, who had once startled the parish by her sudden flight; and she, although she longed to open her heart to them, let no word fall to betray her real character. Her conscience accused her of playing a false part, but for her son's sake she kept silent.

Then, one day,--it was the second Sunday after their arrival,--she rose early in the morning, and asked Thomas to accompany her on a walk up through the valley. There was Sabbath in the air; the soft breath of summer, laden with the perfume of fresh leaves and field-flowers, gently wafted into their faces. The sun glittered in the dewy grass, the crickets sung with a remote voice of wonder, and the air seemed to be half visible, and moved in trembling wavelets on the path before them. Resting on her son's arm, Brita walked slowly up through the flowering meadows; she hardly knew whither her feet bore her, but her heart beat violently, and she often was obliged to pause and press her hands against her bosom, as if to stay the turbulent emotions.

"You are not well, mother," said the son. "It was imprudent in me to allow you to exert yourself in this way."

"Let us sit down on this stone," answered she. "I shall soon be better. Do not look so anxiously at me. Indeed, I am not sick."

He spread his light summer coat on the stone and carefully seated her. She lifted her veil and raised her eyes to the large red-roofed mansion, whose dark outlines drew themselves dimly on the dusky background of the pine forest. Was he still alive, he whose life-hope she had wrecked, he who had once driven her out into the night with all but a curse upon his lips? How would he receive her, if she were to return? Ah, she knew him, and she trembled at the very thought of meeting him. But was not the guilt hers? Could she depart from this valley, could she die in peace, without having thrown herself at his feet and implored his forgiveness? And there, on the opposite side of the valley, lay the home of him who had been the cause of all her misery. What had been his fate, and did he still remember those long happy summer days, ah! so long, long ago? She had dared to ask no questions of the people with whom she lived, but now a sudden weakness had overtaken her, and she felt that to-day must decide her fate; she could no longer bear this torture of uncertainty. Thomas remained standing at her side and looked at her with anxiety and wonder. He knew that she had concealed many things from him, but whatever her reasons might be, he was confident that they were just and weighty. It was not for him to question her about what he might have no right to know. He felt as if he had never loved her as in this moment, when she seemed to be most in need of him, and an overwhelming tenderness took possession of his heart. He suddenly stooped down, took her pale, thin face between his hands and kissed her. The long pent-up emotion burst forth in a flood of tears; she buried her face in her lap and wept long and silently. Then the church-bells began to peal down in the valley, and the slow mighty sound floated calmly and solemnly up to them. How many long-forgotten memories of childhood and youth did they not wake in her bosom--memories of the time when the merry Glitter-Brita, decked with her shining brooches, wended her way to the church among the gayly-dressed lads and maidens of the parish?

A cluster of white-stemmed birches threw its shadow over the stone where the penitent mother was sitting, and the tall grass on both sides of the path nearly hid her from sight. Presently the church-folk began to appear, and Brita raised her head and drew her veil down over her face. No one passed without greeting the strangers, and the women and maidens, according to old fashion, stopped and courtesied. At last, there came an old white-haired man, leaning on the arm of a middle-aged woman. His whole figure was bent forward, and he often stopped and drew his breath heavily.

"Oh, yes, yes," he said, ill a hoarse, broken voice, as he passed before them, "age is gaining on me fast. I can't move about any more as of old. But to church I must this day. God help me! I have done much wrong and need to pray for forgiveness."

"You had better sit down and rest, father," said the woman. "Here is a stone, and the fine lady, I am sure, will allow a weak old man to sit down beside her."

Thomas rose and made a sign to the old man to take his seat.

"O yes, yes," he went on murmuring, as if talking to himself. "Much wrong--much forgiveness. God help us all--miserable sinners. He who hateth not father and mother--and daughter is not worthy of me. O, yes--yes--God comfort us all. Help me up, Grimhild. I think I can move on again, now."

Thomas, of course, did not understand a word of what he said, but seeing that he wished to rise, he willingly offered his assistance, supported his arm and raised him.

"Thanks to you, young man," said the peasant. "And may God reward your kindness."

And the two, father and daughter, moved on, slowly and laboriously, as they had come. Thomas stood following them with his eyes, until a low, half-stifled moan suddenly called him to his mother's side. Her frame trembled violently.

"Mother, mother," implored he, stooping over her, "what has happened? Why are you no more yourself?"

"Ah, my son, I can bear it no longer," sobbed she. "God forgive me--thou must know it all."

He sat down at her side and drew her closely up to him and she hid her face on his bosom. There was a long silence, only broken by the loud chirruping of the crickets.

"My son," she began at last, still hiding her face, "thou art a child of guilt."

"That has been no secret to me, mother," answered he, gravely and tenderly, "since I was old enough to know what guilt was."

She quickly raised her head, and a look of amazement, of joyous surprise, shone through the tears that veiled her eyes. She could read nothing but filial love and confidence in those grave, manly features, and she saw in that moment that all her doubts had been groundless, that her long prayerful struggle had been for naught.

"I brought thee into the world nameless," she whispered, "and thou hast no word of reproach for me?"

"With God's help, I am strong enough to conquer a name for myself, mother," was his answer.

It was the very words of her own secret wish, and upon his lips they sounded like a blessed assurance, like a miraculous fulfillment of her motherly prayer.

"Still, another thing, my child," she went on in a more confident voice. "This is thy native land,--and the old man who was just sitting here at my side was--my father."

And there, in the shadow of the birch-trees, in the summer stillness of that hour, she told him the story of her love, of her flight, and of the misery of these long, toilsome five and twenty years.

Late in the afternoon, Brita and her son were seen returning to the farm-house. A calm, subdued happiness beamed from the mother's countenance; she was again at peace with the world and herself, and her heart was as light as in the days of her early youth. But her bodily strength had given out, and her limbs almost refused to support her. The strain upon her nerves and the constant effort had hitherto enabled her to keep up, but now, when that strain was removed, exhausted nature claimed its right. The next day--she could not leave her bed, and with every hour her strength failed. A physician was sent for. He gave medicine, but no hope. He shook his head gravely, as he went, and both mother and son knew what that meant.

Toward evening, Bjarne Blakstad was summoned, and came at once. Thomas left the room, as the old man entered, and what passed in that hour between father and daughter, only God knows. When the door was again opened, Brita's eyes shone with a strange brilliancy, and Bjarne lay on his knees before the bed, pressing her hand convulsively between both of his.

"This is my son, father," said she, in a language which her son did not understand; and a faint smile of motherly pride and happiness flitted over her pale features. "I would give him to thee in return for what thou hast lost; but God has laid his future in another land."

Bjarne rose, grasped his grandson's hand, and pressed it; and two heavy tears ran down his furrowed cheeks. "Alas," murmured he, "my son, that we should meet thus."

There they stood, bound together by the bonds of blood, but, alas, there lay a world between them.

All night they sat together at the dying woman's bedside. Not a word was spoken. Toward morning, as the sun stole into the darkened chamber, Brita murmured their names, and they laid their hands in hers.

"God be praised," whispered she, scarcely audibly, "I have found you both--my father and my son." A deep pallor spread over her countenance. She was dead.

Two days later, when the body was laid out, Thomas stood alone in the room. The windows were covered with white sheets, and a subdued light fell upon the pale, lifeless countenance. Death had dealt gently with her, she seemed younger than before, and her light wavy hair fell softly over the white forehead. Then there came a middle-aged man, with a dull eye, and a broad forehead, and timidly approached the lonely mourner. He walked on tip-toe and his figure stooped heavily.

For a long while he stood gazing at the dead body, then he knelt down at the foot of the coffin, and began to sob violently. At last he arose, took two steps toward the young man, paused again, and departed silently as he had come. It was Halvard.

Close under the wall of the little red-painted church, they dug the grave; and a week later her father was laid to rest at his daughter's side.

But the fresh winds blew over the Atlantic and beckoned the son to new fields of labor in the great land of the future.

A GOOD-FOR-NOTHING.

RALPH GRIM was born a gentleman. He had the misfortune of coming into the world some ten years later than might reasonably have been expected. Colonel Grim and his lady had celebrated twelve anniversaries of their wedding-day, and had given up all hopes of ever having a son and heir, when this late-comer startled them by his unexpected appearance. The only previous addition to the family had been a daughter, and she was then ten summers old.

Ralph was a very feeble child, and could only with great difficulty be persuaded to retain his hold of the slender thread which bound him to existence. He was rubbed with whisky, and wrapped in cotton, and given mare's milk to drink, and God knows what not, and the Colonel swore a round oath of paternal delight when at last the infant stopped gasping in that distressing way and began to breathe like other human beings. The mother, who, in spite of her anxiety for the child's life, had found time to plot for him a career of future magnificence, now suddenly set him apart for literature, because that was the easiest road to fame, and disposed of him in marriage to one of the most distinguished families of the land. She cautiously suggested this to her husband when he came to take his seat at her bedside; but to her utter astonishment she found that he had been indulging a similar train of thought, and had already destined the infant prodigy for the army. She, however, could not give up her predilection for literature, and the Colonel, who could not bear to be contradicted in his own house, as he used to say, was getting every minute louder and more flushed, when, happily, the doctor's arrival interrupted the dispute.

As Ralph grew up from infancy to childhood, he began to give decided promise of future distinction. He was fond of sitting down in a corner and sucking his thumb, which his mother interpreted as the sign of that brooding disposition peculiar to poets and men of lofty genius. At the age of five, he had become sole master in the house. He slapped his sister Hilda in the face, or pulled her hair, when she hesitated to obey him, tyrannized over his nurse, and sternly refused to go to bed in spite of his mother's entreaties. On such occasions, the Colonel would hide his face behind his newspaper, and chuckle with delight; it was evident that nature had intended his son for a great military commander. As soon as Ralph himself was old enough to have any thoughts about his future destiny, he made up his mind that he would like to be a pirate. A few months later, having contracted an immoderate taste for candy, he contented himself with the comparatively humble position of a baker; but when he had read "Robinson Crusoe," he manifested a strong desire to go to sea in the hope of being wrecked on some desolate island. The parents spent long evenings gravely discussing these indications of uncommon genius, and each interpreted them in his or her own way.

"He is not like any other child I ever knew," said the mother.

"To be sure," responded the father, earnestly. "He is a most extraordinary child. I was a very remarkable child too, even if I do say it myself; but, as far as I remember, I never aspired to being wrecked on an uninhabited is land."

The Colonel probably spoke the truth; but he forgot to take into account that he had never read "Robinson Crusoe."

Of Ralph's school-days there is but little to report, for, to tell the truth, he did not fancy going to school, as the discipline annoyed him. The day after his having entered the gymnasium, which was to prepare him for the Military Academy, the principal saw him waiting at the gate after his class had been dismissed. He approached him, and asked why he did not go home with the rest.

"I am waiting for the servant to carry my books," was the boy's answer.

"Give me your books," said the teacher.

Ralph reluctantly obeyed. That day the Colonel was not a little surprised to see his son marching up the street, and every now and then glancing behind him with a look of discomfort at the principal, who was following quietly in his train, carrying a parcel of school-books. Colonel Grim and his wife, divining the teacher's intention, agreed that it was a great outrage, but they did not mention the matter to Ralph. Henceforth, however, the boy refused to be accompanied by his servant. A week later he was impudent to the teacher of gymnastics, who whipped him in return. The Colonel's rage knew no bounds; he rode in great haste to the gymnasium, reviled the teacher for presuming to chastise HIS son, and committed the boy to the care of a private tutor.

At the age of sixteen, Ralph went to the capital with the intention of entering the Military Academy. He was a tall, handsome youth, slender of stature, and carried himself as erect as a candle. He had a light, clear complexion of almost feminine delicacy; blonde, curly hair, which he always kept carefully brushed; a low forehead, and a straight, finely modeled nose. There was an expression of extreme sensitiveness about the nostrils, and a look of indolence in the dark-blue eyes. But the ensemble of his features was pleasing, his dress irreproachable, and his manners bore no trace of the awkward self-consciousness peculiar to his age. Immediately on his arrival in the capital he hired a suite of rooms in the aristocratic part of the city, and furnished them rather expensively, but in excellent taste. From a bosom friend, whom he met by accident in the restaurant's pavilion in the park, he learned that a pair of antlers, a stuffed eagle, or falcon, and a couple of swords, were indispensable to a well-appointed apartment. He accordingly bought these articles at a curiosity-shop. During the first weeks of his residence in the city he made some feeble efforts to perfect himself in mathematics, in which he suspected he was somewhat deficient. But when the same officious friend laughed at him, and called him "green," he determined to trust to fortune, and henceforth devoted himself the more assiduously to the French ballet, where he had already made some interesting acquaintances.

The time for the examination came; the French ballet did not prove a good preparation; Ralph failed. It quite shook him for the time, and he felt humiliated. He had not the courage to tell his father; so he lingered on from day to day, sat vacantly gazing out of his window, and tried vainly to interest himself in the busy bustle down on the street. It provoked him that everybody else should be so light-hearted, when he was, or at least fancied himself, in trouble. The parlor grew intolerable; he sought refuge in his bedroom. There he sat one evening (it was the third day after the examination), and stared out upon the gray stone walls which on all sides enclosed the narrow court-yard. The round stupid face of the moon stood tranquilly dozing like a great Limburger cheese suspended under the sky.

Ralph, at least, could think of a no more fitting simile. But the bright-eyed young girl in the window hard by sent a longing look up to the same moon, and thought of her distant home on the fjords, where the glaciers stood like hoary giants, and caught the yellow moonbeams on their glittering shields of snow. She had been reading "Ivanhoe" all the afternoon, until the twilight had overtaken her quite unaware, and now she suddenly remembered that she had forgotten to write her German exercise. She lifted her face and saw a pair of sad, vacant eyes, gazing at her from the next window in the angle of the court. She was a little startled at first, but in the next moment she thought of her German exercise and took heart.

"Do you know German?" she said; then immediately repented that she had said it.

"I do," was the answer.

She took up her apron and began to twist it with an air of embarrassment.

"I didn't mean anything," she whispered, at last. "I only wanted to know."

"You are very kind."

That answer roused her; he was evidently making sport of her.

"Well, then, if you do, you may write my exercise for me. I have marked the place in the book."

And she flung her book over to his window, and he caught it on the edge of the sill, just as it was falling.

"You are a very strange girl," he remarked, turning over the leaves of the book, although it was too dark to read. "How old are you?"

"I shall be fourteen six weeks before Christmas," answered she, frankly.

"Then I excuse you."

"No, indeed," cried she, vehemently. "You needn't excuse me at all. If you don't want to write my exercise, you may send the book back again. I am very sorry I spoke to you, and I shall never do it again."

"But you will not get the book back again without the exercise," replied he, quietly. "Good-night."

The girl stood long looking after him, hoping that he would return. Then, with a great burst of repentance, she hid her face in her lap, and began to cry.

"Oh, dear, I didn't mean to be rude," she sobbed. "But it was Ivanhoe and Rebecca who upset me."

The next morning she was up before daylight, and waited for two long hours in great suspense before the curtain of his window was raised. He greeted her politely; threw a hasty glance around the court to see if he was observed, and then tossed her book dexterously over into her hands.

"I have pinned the written exercise to the fly-leaf," he said. "You will probably have time to copy it before breakfast."

"I am ever so much obliged to you," she managed to stammer.

He looked so tall and handsome, and grown-up, and her remorse stuck in her throat, and threatened to choke her. She had taken him for a boy as he sat there in his window the evening before.

"By the way, what is your name?" he asked, carelessly, as he turned to go.

"Bertha."

"Well, my dear Bertha, I am happy to have made your acquaintance."

And he again made her a polite bow, and entered his parlor.

"How provokingly familiar he is," thought she; "but no one can deny that he is handsome."

The bright roguish face of the young girl haunted Ralph during the whole next week. He had been in love at least ten times before, of course; but, like most boys, with young ladies far older than himself. He found himself frequently glancing over to her window in the hope of catching another glimpse of her face; but the curtain was always drawn down, and Bertha remained invisible. During the second week, however, she relented, and they had many a pleasant chat together. He now volunteered to write all her exercises, and she made no objections. He learned that she was the daughter of a well-to-do peasant in the sea-districts of Norway (and it gave him quite a shock to hear it), and that she was going to school in the city, and boarded with an old lady who kept a pension in the house adjoining the one in which he lived.

One day in the autumn Ralph was surprised by the sudden arrival of his father, and the fact of his failure in the examination could no longer be kept a secret. The old Colonel flared up at once when Ralph made his confession; the large veins upon his forehead swelled; he grew coppery-red in his face, and stormed up and down the floor, until his son became seriously alarmed; but, to his great relief, he was soon made aware that his father's wrath was not turned against him personally, but against the officials of the Military Academy who had rejected him. The Colonel took it as an insult to his own good name and irreproachable standing as an officer; he promptly refused any other explanation, and vainly racked his brain to remember if any youthful folly of his could possibly have made him enemies among the teachers of the Academy. He at last felt satisfied that it was envy of his own greatness and rapid advancement which had induced the rascals to take vengeance on his son. Ralph reluctantly followed his father back to the country town where the latter was stationed, and the fair-haired Bertha vanished from his horizon. His mother's wish now prevailed, and he began, in his own easy way, to prepare himself for the University. He had little taste for Cicero, and still less for Virgil, but with the use of a "pony" he soon gained sufficient knowledge of these authors to be able to talk in a sort of patronizing way about them, to the great delight of his fond parents. He took quite a fancy, however, to the ode in Horace ending with the lines:

Dulce ridentem, Dulce loquentem, Lalagen amabo.

And in his thought he substituted for Lalage the fair-haired Bertha, quite regardless of the requirements of the metre.

To make a long story short, three years later Ralph returned to the capital, and, after having worn out several tutors, actually succeeded in entering the University.

The first year of college life is a happy time to every young man, and Ralph enjoyed its processions, its parliamentary gatherings, and its leisure, as well as the rest. He was certainly not the man to be sentimental over the loss of a young girl whom, moreover, he had only known for a few weeks. Nevertheless, he thought of her at odd times, but not enough to disturb his pleasure. The standing of his family, his own handsome appearance, and his immaculate linen opened to him the best houses of the city, and he became a great favorite in society. At lectures he was seldom seen, but more frequently in the theatres, where he used to come in during the middle of the first act, take his station in front of the orchestra box, and eye, through his lorgnettes, by turns, the actresses and the ladies of the parquet.

II.

Two months passed, and then came the great annual ball which the students give at the opening of the second semester. Ralph was a man of importance that evening; first, because he belonged to a great family; secondly, because he was the handsomest man of his year. He wore a large golden star on his breast (for his fellow-students had made him a Knight of the Golden Boar), and a badge of colored ribbons in his button-hole.

The ball was a brilliant affair, and everybody was in excellent spirits, especially the ladies. Ralph danced incessantly, twirled his soft mustache, and uttered amiable platitudes. It was toward midnight, just as the company was moving out to supper, that he caught the glance of a pair of dark-blue eyes, which suddenly drove the blood to his cheeks and hastened the beating of his heart. But when he looked once more the dark-blue eyes were gone, and his unruly heart went on hammering against his side. He laid his hand on his breast and glanced furtively at his fair neighbor, but she looked happy and unconcerned, for the flavor of the ice-cream was delicious. It seemed an endless meal, but, when it was done, Ralph rose, led his partner back to the ball-room, and hastily excused himself. His glance wandered round the wide hall, seeking the well-remembered eyes once more, and, at length, finding them in a remote corner, half hid behind a moving wall of promenaders. In another moment he was at Bertha's side.

"You must have been purposely hiding yourself, Miss Bertha," said he, when the usual greetings were exchanged. "I have not caught a glimpse of you all this evening, until a few moments ago."

"But I have seen you all the while," answered the girl, frankly. "I knew you at once as I entered the hall."

"If I had but known that you were here," resumed Ralph, as it were, invisibly expanding with an agreeable sense of dignity, "I assure you, you would have been the very first one I should have sought."

She raised her large grave eyes to his, as if questioning his sincerity; but she made no answer.

"Good gracious!" thought Ralph. "She takes things terribly in earnest."

"You look so serious, Miss Bertha," said he, after a moment's pause. "I remember you as a bright-eyed, flaxen-haired little girl, who threw her German exercise-book to me across the yard, and whose merry laughter still rings pleasantly in my memory. I confess I don't find it quite easy to identify this grave young lady with my merry friend of three years ago."

"In other words, you are disappointed at not finding me the same as I used to be."

"No, not exactly that; but--"

Ralph paused and looked puzzled. There was something in the earnestness of her manner which made a facetious compliment seem grossly inappropriate, and in the moment no other escape suggested itself.

"But what?" demanded Bertha, mercilessly.

"Have you ever lost an old friend?" asked he, abruptly.

"Yes; how so?"

"Then," answered he, while his features lighted up with a happy inspiration--"then you will appreciate my situation. I fondly cherished my old picture of you in my memory. Now I have lost it, and I cannot help regretting the loss. I do not mean, however, to imply that this new acquaintance--this second edition of yourself, so to speak--will prove less interesting."

She again sent him a grave, questioning look, and began to gaze intently upon the stone in her bracelet.

"I suppose you will laugh at me," began she, while a sudden blush flitted over her countenance. "But this is my first ball, and I feel as if I had rushed into a whirl-pool, from which I have, since the first rash plunge was made, been vainly trying to escape. I feel so dreadfully forlorn. I hardly know anybody here except my cousin, who invited me, and I hardly think I know him either."

"Well, since you are irredeemably committed," replied Ralph, as the music, after some prefatory flourishes, broke into the delicious rhythm of a Strauss waltz, "then it is no use struggling against fate. Come, let us make the plunge together. Misery loves company."

He offered her his arm, and she arose, somewhat hesitatingly, and followed.

"I am afraid," she whispered, as they fell into line with the procession that was moving down the long hall, "that you have asked me to dance merely because I said I felt forlorn. If that is the case, I should prefer to be led back to my seat."

"What a base imputation!" cried Ralph.

There was something so charmingly naive in this self-depreciation-- something so altogether novel in his experience, and, he could not help adding, just a little bit countrified. His spirits rose; he began to relish keenly his position as an experienced man of the world, and, in the agreeable glow of patronage and conscious superiority, chatted with hearty ABANDON with his little rustic beauty.

"If your dancing is as perfect as your German exercises were," said she, laughing, as they swung out upon the floor, "then I promise myself a good deal of pleasure from our meeting."

"Never fear," answered he, quickly reversing his step, and whirling with many a capricious turn away among the thronging couples.

When Ralph drove home in his carriage toward morning he briefly summed up his impressions of Bertha in the following adjectives: intelligent, delightfully unsophisticated, a little bit verdant, but devilish pretty.

Some weeks later Colonel Grim received an appointment at the fortress of Aggershuus, and immediately took up his residence in the capital. He saw that his son cut a fine figure in the highest circles of society, and expressed his gratification in the most emphatic terms. If he had known, however, that Ralph was in the habit of visiting, with alarming regularity, at the house of a plebeian merchant in a somewhat obscure street, he would, no doubt, have been more chary of his praise. But the Colonel suspected nothing, and it was well for the peace of the family that he did not. It may have been cowardice in Ralph that he never mentioned Bertha's name to his family or to his aristocratic acquaintances; for, to be candid, he himself felt ashamed of the power she exerted over him, and by turns pitied and ridiculed himself for pursuing so inglorious a conquest. Nevertheless it wounded his egotism that she never showed any surprise at seeing him, that she received him with a certain frank unceremoniousness, which, however, was very becoming to her; that she invariably went on with her work heedless of his presence, and in everything treated him as if she had been his equal. She persisted in talking with him in a half sisterly fashion about his studies and his future career, warned him with great solicitude against some of his reprobate friends, of whose merry adventures he had told her; and if he ventured to compliment her on her beauty or her accomplishments, she would look up gravely from her sewing, or answer him in a way which seemed to banish the idea of love-making into the land of the impossible. He was constantly tormented by the suspicion that she secretly disapproved of him, and that from a mere moral interest in his welfare she was conscientiously laboring to make him a better man. Day after day he parted from her feeling humiliated, faint-hearted, and secretly indignant both at himself and her, and day after day he returned only to renew the same experience. At last it became too intolerable, he could endure it no longer. Let it make or break, certainty, at all risks, was at least preferable to this sickening suspense. That he loved her, he could no longer doubt; let his parents foam and fret as much as they pleased; for once he was going to stand on his own legs. And in the end, he thought, they would have to yield, for they had no son but him.

Bertha was going to return to her home on the sea-coast in a week. Ralph stood in the little low-ceiled parlor, as she imagined, to bid her good-bye. They had been speaking of her father, her brothers, and the farm, and she had expressed the wish that if he ever should come to that part of the country he might pay them a visit. Her words had kindled a vague hope in his breast, but in their very frankness and friendly regard there was something which slew the hope they had begotten. He held her hand in his, and her large confiding eyes shone with an emotion which was beautiful, but was yet not love.

"If you were but a peasant born like myself," said she, in a voice which sounded almost tender, "then I should like to talk to you as I would to my own brother; but--"

"No, not brother, Bertha," cried he, with sudden vehemence; "I love you better than I ever loved any earthly being, and if you knew how firmly this love has clutched at the roots of my heart, you would perhaps--you would at least not look so reproachfully at me."

She dropped his hand, and stood for a moment silent.

"I am sorry that it should have come to this, Mr. Grim," said she, visibly struggling for calmness. "And I am perhaps more to blame than you."

"Blame," muttered he, "why are you to blame?"

"Because I do not love you; although I sometimes feared that this might come.

But then again I persuaded myself that it could not be so."

He took a step toward the door, laid his hand on the knob, and gazed down before him.

"Bertha," began he, slowly, raising his head, "you have always disapproved of me, you have despised me in your heart, but you thought you would be doing a good work if you succeeded in making a man of me."

"You use strong language," answered she, hesitatingly; "but there is truth in what you say."

Again there was a long pause, in which the ticking of the old parlor clock grew louder and louder.

"Then," he broke out at last, "tell me before we part if I can do nothing to gain--I will not say your love--but only your regard? What would you do if you were in my place?"

"My advice you will hardly heed, and I do not even know that it would be well if you did. But if I were a man in your position, I should break with my whole past, start out into the world where nobody knew me, and where I should be dependent only upon my own strength, and there I would conquer a place for myself, if it were only for the satisfaction of knowing that I was really a man. Here cushions are sewed under your arms, a hundred invisible threads bind you to a life of idleness and vanity, everybody is ready to carry you on his hands, the road is smoothed for you, every stone carefully moved out of your path, and you will probably go to your grave without having ever harbored one earnest thought, without having done one manly deed."

Ralph stood transfixed, gazing at her with open mouth; he felt a kind of stupid fright, as if some one had suddenly seized him by the shoulders and shaken him violently. He tried vainly to remove his eyes from Bertha. She held him as by a powerful spell. He saw that her face was lighted with an altogether new beauty; he noticed the deep glow upon her cheek, the brilliancy of her eye, the slight quiver of her lip. But he saw all this as one sees things in a half-trance, without attempting to account for them; the door between his soul and his senses was closed.

"I know that I have been bold in speaking to you in this way," she said at last, seating herself in a chair at the window. "But it was yourself who asked me. And I have felt all the time that I should have to tell you this before we parted."

"And," answered he, making a strong effort to appear calm, "if I follow your advice, will you allow me to see you once more before you go?"

"I shall remain here another week, and shall, during that time, always be ready to receive you."

"Thank you. Good-bye."

"Good-bye."

Ralph carefully avoided all the fashionable thoroughfares; he felt degraded before himself, and he had an idea that every man could read his humiliation in his countenance. Now he walked on quickly, striking the sidewalk with his heels; now, again, he fell into an uneasy, reckless saunter, according as the changing moods inspired defiance of his sentence, or a qualified surrender. And, as he walked on, the bitterness grew within him, and he pitilessly reviled himself for having allowed himself to be made a fool of by "that little country goose," when he was well aware that there were hundreds of women of the best families of the land who would feel honored at receiving his attentions. But this sort of reasoning he knew to be both weak and contemptible, and his better self soon rose in loud rebellion.

"After all," he muttered, "in the main thing she was right. I am a miserable good-for-nothing, a hot-house plant, a poor stick, and if I were a woman myself, I don't think I should waste my affections on a man of that calibre."

Then he unconsciously fell to analyzing Bertha's character, wondering vaguely that a person who moved so timidly in social life, appearing so diffident, from an ever-present fear of blundering against the established forms of etiquette, could judge so quickly, and with such a merciless certainty, whenever a moral question, a question of right and wrong, was at issue. And, pursuing the same train of thought, he contrasted her with himself, who moved in the highest spheres of society as in his native element, heedless of moral scruples, and conscious of no loftier motive for his actions than the immediate pleasure of the moment.

As Ralph turned the corner of a street, he heard himself hailed from the other sidewalk by a chorus of merry voices.

"Ah, my dear Baroness," cried a young man, springing across the street and grasping Ralph's hand (all his student friends called him the Baroness), "in the name of this illustrious company, allow me to salute you. But why the deuce--what is the matter with you? If you have the Katzenjammer, [7] soda-water is the thing. Come along,--it's my treat!"

The students instantly thronged around Ralph, who stood distractedly swinging his cane and smiling idiotically.

"I am not quite well," said he; "leave me alone."

"No, to be sure, you don't look well," cried a jolly youth, against whom Bertha had frequently warned him; "but a glass of sherry will soon restore you. It would be highly immoral to leave you in this condition without taking care of you."

Ralph again vainly tried to remonstrate; but the end was, that he reluctantly followed.

He had always been a conspicuous figure in the student world; but that night he astonished his friends by his eloquence, his reckless humor, and his capacity for drinking. He made a speech for "Woman," which bristled with wit, cynicism, and sarcastic epigrams. One young man, named Vinter, who was engaged, undertook to protest against his sweeping condemnation, and declared that Ralph, who was a Universal favorite among the ladies, ought to be the last to revile them.

"If," he went on, "the Baroness should propose to six well-known ladies here in this city whom I could mention, I would wager six Johannisbergers, and an equal amount of champagne, that every one of them would accept him."

The others loudly applauded this proposal, and Ralph accepted the wager. The letters were written on the spot, and immediately dispatched. Toward morning, the merry carousal broke up, and Ralph was conducted in triumph to his home.

III.

Two days later, Ralph again knocked on Bertha's door. He looked paler than usual, almost haggard; his immaculate linen was a little crumpled, and he carried no cane; his lips were tightly compressed, and his face wore an air of desperate resolution.

"It is done," he said, as he seated himself opposite her. "I am going."

"Going!" cried she, startled at his unusual appearance. "How, where?"

"To America. I sail to-night. I have followed your advice, you see. I have cut off the last bridge behind me."

"But, Ralph," she exclaimed, in a voice of alarm. "Something dreadful must have happened. Tell me quick; I must know it."

"No; nothing dreadful," muttered he, smiling bitterly. "I have made a little scandal, that is all. My father told me to-day to go to the devil, if I chose, and my mother gave me five hundred dollars to help me along on the way. If you wish to know, here is the explanation."

And he pulled from his pocket six perfumed and carefully folded notes, and threw them into her lap.

"Do you wish me to read them?" she asked, with growing surprise.

"Certainly. Why not?"

She hastily opened one note after the other, and read.

"But, Ralph," she cried, springing up from her seat, while her eyes flamed with indignation, "what does this mean? What have you done?"

"I didn't think it needed any explanation," replied he, with feigned indifference. "I proposed to them all, and, you see, they all accepted me. I received all these letters to-day. I only wished to know whether the whole world regarded me as such a worthless scamp as you told me I was."

She did not answer, but sat mutely staring at him, fiercely crumpling a rose-colored note in her hand. He began to feel uncomfortable under her gaze, and threw himself about uneasily in his chair.

"Well," said he, at length, rising, "I suppose there is nothing more. Good-bye."

"One moment, Mr. Grim," demanded she, sternly. "Since I have already said so much, and you have obligingly revealed to me a new side of your character, I claim the right to correct the opinion I expressed of you at our last meeting."

"I am all attention."

"I did think, Mr. Grim," began she, breathing hard, and steadying herself against the table at which she stood, "that you were a very selfish man--an embodiment of selfishness, absolute and supreme, but I did not believe that you were wicked."

"And what convinced you that I was selfish, if I may ask?"

"What convinced me?" repeated she, in a tone of inexpressible contempt. "When did you ever act from any generous regard for others? What good did you ever do to anybody?"

"You might ask, with equal justice, what good I ever did to myself."

"In a certain sense, yes; because to gratify a mere momentary wish is hardly doing one's self good."

"Then I have, at all events, followed the Biblical precept, and treated my neighbor very much as I treat myself."

"I did think," continued Bertha, without heeding the remark, "that you were at bottom kind-hearted, but too hopelessly well-bred ever to commit an act of any decided complexion, either good or bad. Now I see that I have misjudged you, and that you are capable of outraging the most sacred feelings of a woman's heart in mere wantonness, or for the sake of satisfying a base curiosity, which never could have entered the mind of an upright and generous man."

The hard, benumbed look in Ralph's face thawed in the warmth of her presence, and her words, though stern, touched a secret spring in his heart. He made two or three vain attempts to speak, then suddenly broke down, and cried:

"Bertha, Bertha, even if you scorn me, have patience with me, and listen."

And he told her, in rapid, broken sentences, how his love for her had grown from day to day, until he could no longer master it; and how, in an unguarded moment, when his pride rose in fierce conflict against his love, he had done this reckless deed of which he was now heartily ashamed. The fervor of his words touched her, for she felt that they were sincere. Large mute tears trembled in her eyelashes as she sat gazing tenderly at him, and in the depth of her soul the wish awoke that she might have been able to return this great and strong love of his; for she felt that in this love lay the germ of a new, of a stronger and better man. She noticed, with a half-regretful pleasure, his handsome figure, his delicately shaped hands, and the noble cast of his features; an overwhelming pity for him rose within her, and she began to reproach herself for having spoken so harshly, and, as she now thought, so unjustly. Perhaps he read in her eyes the unspoken wish. He seized her hand, and his words fell with a warm and alluring cadence upon her ear.

"I shall not see you for a long time to come, Bertha," said he, "but if, at the end of five or six years your hand is still free, and I return another man--a man to whom you could safely intrust your happiness--would you then listen to what I may have to say to you? For I promise, by all that we both hold sacred--"

"No, no," interrupted she, hastily. "Promise nothing. It would be unjust to-yourself, and perhaps also to me; for a sacred promise is a terrible thing, Ralph.

Let us both remain free; and, if you return and still love me, then come, and I shall receive you and listen to you. And even if you have outgrown your love, which is, indeed, more probable, come still to visit me wherever I may be, and we shall meet as friends and rejoice in the meeting."

"You know best," he murmured. "Let it be as you have said."

He arose, took her face between his hands, gazed long and tenderly into her eyes, pressed a kiss upon her forehead, and hastened away.

That night Ralph boarded the steamer for Hull, and three weeks later landed in New York.

IV.

The first three months of Ralph's sojourn in America were spent in vain attempts to obtain a situation. Day after day he walked down Broadway, calling at various places of business and night after night he returned to his cheerless room with a faint heart and declining spirits. It was, after all, a more serious thing than he had imagined, to cut the cable which binds one to the land of one's birth. There a hundred subtle influences, the existence of which no one suspects until the moment they are withdrawn, unite to keep one in the straight path of rectitude, or at least of external respectability; and Ralph's life had been all in society; the opinion of his fellow-men had been the one force to which he implicitly deferred, and the conscience by which he had been wont to test his actions had been nothing but the aggregate judgment of his friends. To such a man the isolation and the utter irresponsibility of a life among strangers was tenfold more dangerous; and Ralph found, to his horror, that his character contained innumerable latent possibilities which the easygoing life in his home probably never would have revealed to him. It often cut him to the quick, when, on entering an office in his daily search for employment, he was met by hostile or suspicious glances, or when, as it occasionally happened, the door was slammed in his face, as if he were a vagabond or an impostor. Then the wolf was often roused within him, and he felt a momentary wild desire to become what the people here evidently believed him to be. Many a night he sauntered irresolutely about the gambling places in obscure streets, and the glare of light, the rude shouts and clamors in the same moment repelled and attracted him. If he went to the devil, who would care? His father had himself pointed out the way to him; and nobody could blame him if he followed the advice. But then again a memory emerged from that chamber of his soul which still he held sacred; and Bertha's deep-blue eyes gazed upon him with their earnest look of tender warning and regret.

When the summer was half gone, Ralph had gained many a hard victory over himself, and learned many a useful lesson; and at length he swallowed his pride, divested himself of his fine clothes, and accepted a position as assistant gardener at a villa on the Hudson. And as he stood perspiring with a spade in his hand, and a cheap broad-brimmed straw hat on his head, he often took a grim pleasure in picturing to himself how his aristocratic friends at home would receive him, if he should introduce himself to them in this new costume.

"After all, it was only my position they cared for," he reflected, bitterly; "without my father's name what would I be to them?"

Then, again, there was a certain satisfaction in knowing that, for his present situation, humble as it was, he was indebted to nobody but himself; and the thought that Bertha's eyes, if they could have seen him now would have dwelt upon him with pleasure and approbation, went far to console him for his aching back, his sunburned face, and his swollen and blistered hands.

One day, as Ralph was raking the gravel-walks in the garden, his employer's daughter, a young lady of seventeen, came out and spoke to him. His culture and refinement of manner struck her with wonder, and she asked him to tell her his history; but then he suddenly grew very grave, and she forbore pressing him. From that time she attached a kind of romantic interest to him, and finally induced her father to obtain him a situation that would be more to his taste. And, before winter came, Ralph saw the dawn of a new future glimmering before him. He had wrestled bravely with fate, and had once more gained a victory. He began the career in which success and distinction awaited him, as proof-reader on a newspaper in the city. He had fortunately been familiar with the English language before he left home, and by the strength of his will he conquered all difficulties. At the end of two years he became attached to the editorial staff; new ambitious hopes, hitherto foreign to his mind, awoke within him; and with joyous tumult of heart he saw life opening its wide vistas before him, and he labored on manfully to repair the losses of the past, and to prepare himself for greater usefulness in times to come. He felt in himself a stronger and fuller manhood, as if the great arteries of the vast universal world-life pulsed in his own being. The drowsy, indolent existence at home appeared like a dull remote dream from which he had awaked, and he blessed the destiny which, by its very sternness, had mercifully saved him; he blessed her, too, who, from the very want of love for him, had, perhaps, made him worthier of love.

The years flew rapidly. Society had flung its doors open to him, and what was more, he had found some warm friends, in whose houses he could come and go at pleasure. He enjoyed keenly the privilege of daily association with high-minded and refined women; their eager activity of intellect stimulated him, their exquisite ethereal grace and their delicately chiseled beauty satisfied his aesthetic cravings, and the responsive vivacity of their nature prepared him ever new surprises. He felt a strange fascination in the presence of these women, and the conviction grew upon him that their type of womanhood was superior to any he had hitherto known. And by way of refuting his own argument, he would draw from his pocket-book the photograph of Bertha, which had a secret compartment there all to itself, and, gazing tenderly at it, would eagerly defend her against the disparaging reflections which the involuntary comparison had provoked. And still, how could he help seeing that her features, though well molded, lacked animation; that her eye, with its deep, trustful glance, was not brilliant, and that the calm earnestness of her face, when compared with the bright, intellectual beauty of his present friends, appeared pale and simple, like a violet in a bouquet of vividly colored roses? It gave him a quick pang, when, at times, he was forced to admit this; nevertheless, it was the truth.

After six years of residence in America, Ralph had gained a very high reputation as a journalist of rare culture and ability, and, in 1867 he was sent to the World's Exhibition in Paris, as correspondent of the paper on which he had during all these years been employed. What wonder, then, that he started for Europe a few weeks before his presence was needed in the imperial city, and that he steered his course directly toward the fjord valley where Bertha had her home? It was she who had bidden him Godspeed when he fled from the land of his birth, and she, too, should receive his first greeting on his return.

V.

The sun had fortified itself behind a citadel of flaming clouds, and the upper forest region shone with a strange ethereal glow, while the lower plains were wrapped in shadow; but the shadow itself had a strong suffusion of color. The mountain peaks rose cold and blue in the distance.

Ralph, having inquired his way of the boatman who had landed him at the pier, walked rapidly along the beach, with a small valise in his hand, and a light summer overcoat flung over his shoulder. Many half-thoughts grazed his mind, and ere the first had taken shape, the second, and the third came and chased it away. And still they all in some fashion had reference to Bertha; for in a misty, abstract way, she filled his whole mind; but for some indefinable reason, he was afraid to give free rein to the sentiment which lurked in the remoter corners of his soul.

Onward he hastened, while his heart throbbed with the quickening tempo of mingled expectation and fear. Now and then one of those chill gusts of air which seem to be careering about aimlessly in the atmosphere during early summer, would strike into his face, and recall him to a keener self-consciousness.

Ralph concluded, from his increasing agitation, that he must be very near Bertha's home. He stopped and looked around him. He saw a large maple at the roadside, some thirty steps from where he was standing, and the girl who was sitting under it, resting her head in her hand and gazing out over the sea, he recognized in an instant to be Bertha. He sprang up on the road, not crossing, however, her line of vision, and approached her noiselessly from behind.

"Bertha," he whispered.

She gave a little joyous cry, sprang up, and made a gesture as if to throw herself in his arms; then suddenly checked herself, blushed crimson, and moved a step backward.

"You came so suddenly," she murmured.

"But, Bertha," cried he (and the full bass of his voice rang through her very soul), "have I gone into exile and waited these many years for so cold a welcome?"

"You have changed so much, Ralph," she answered, with that old grave smile which he knew so well, and stretched out both her hands toward him. "And I have thought of you so much since you went away, and blamed myself because I had judged you so harshly, and wondered that you could listen to me so patiently, and never bear me any malice for what I said."

"If you had said a word less," declared Ralph, seating himself at her side on the greensward, "or if you had varnished it over with politeness, then you would probably have failed to produce any effect and I should not have been burdened with that heavy debt of gratitude which I now owe you. I was a pretty thick-skinned animal in those days, Bertha. You said the right word at the right moment; you gave me a hold and a good piece of advice, which my own ingenuity would never have suggested to me. I will not thank you, because, in so grave a case as this, spoken thanks sound like a mere mockery. Whatever I am, Bertha, and whatever I may hope to be, I owe it all to that hour."

She listened with rapture to the manly assurance of his voice; her eyes dwelt with unspeakable joy upon his strong, bronzed features, his full thick blonde beard, and the vigorous proportions of his frame. Many and many a time during his absence had she wondered how he would look if he ever came back, and with that minute conscientiousness which, as it were, pervaded her whole character, she had held herself responsible before God for his fate, prayed for him, and trembled lest evil powers should gain the ascendency over his soul.

On their way to the house they talked together of many things, but in a guarded, cautious fashion, and without the cheerful abandonment of former years. They both, as it were, groped their way carefully in each other's minds, and each vaguely felt that there was something in the other's thought which it was not well to touch unbidden. Bertha saw that all her fears for him had been groundless, and his very appearance lifted the whole weight of responsibility from her breast; and still, did she rejoice at her deliverance from her burden? Ah, no, in this moment she knew that that which she had foolishly cherished as the best and noblest part of herself, had been but a selfish need of her own heart. She feared that she had only taken that interest in him which one feels in a thing of one's own making; and now, when she saw that he had risen quite above her; that he was free and strong, and could have no more need of her, she had, instead of generous pleasure at his success, but a painful sense of emptiness, as if something very dear had been taken from her.

Ralph, too, was loath to analyze the impression his old love made upon him. His feelings were of so complex a nature, he was anxious to keep his more magnanimous impulses active, and he strove hard to convince himself that she was still the same to him as she had been before they had ever parted. But, alas! though the heart be warm and generous, the eye is a merciless critic. And the man who had moved on the wide arena of the world, whose mind had housed the large thoughts of this century, and expanded with its invigorating breath,--was he to blame because he had unconsciously outgrown his old provincial self, and could no more judge by its standards?

Bertha's father was a peasant, but he had, by his lumber trade, acquired what in Norway was called a very handsome fortune. He received his guest with dignified reserve, and Ralph thought he detected in his eyes a lurking look of distrust. "I know your errand," that look seemed to say, "but you had better give it up at once. It will be of no use for you to try."

And after supper, as Ralph and Bertha sat talking confidingly with each other at the window, he sent his daughter a quick, sharp glance, and then, without ceremony, commanded her to go to bed. Ralph's heart gave a great thump within him; not because he feared the old man, but because his words, as well as his glances, revealed to him the sad history of these long, patient years. He doubted no longer that the love which he had once so ardently desired was his at last; and he made a silent vow that, come what might, he would remain faithful.

As he came down to breakfast the next morning, he found Bertha sitting at the window, engaged in hemming what appeared to be a rough kitchen towel. She bent eagerly over her work, and only a vivid flush upon her cheek told him that she had noticed his coming. He took a chair, seated himself opposite her, and bade her "good-morning." She raised her head, and showed him a sweet, troubled countenance, which the early sunlight illumined with a high spiritual beauty. It reminded him forcibly of those pale, sweet-faced saints of Fra Angelico, with whom the frail flesh seems ever on the point of yielding to the ardent aspirations of the spirit. And still, even in this moment he could not prevent his eyes from observing that one side of her forefinger was rough from sewing, and that the whiteness of her arm, which the loose sleeves displayed, contrasted strongly with the browned and sunburned complexion of her hands.

After breakfast they again walked together on the beach, and Ralph, having once formed his resolution, now talked freely of the New World--of his sphere of activity there; of his friends and of his plans for the future; and she listened to him with a mild, perplexed look in her eyes, as if trying vainly to follow the flight of his thoughts. And he wondered, with secret dismay, whether she was still the same strong, brave-hearted girl whom he had once accounted almost bold; whether the life in this narrow valley, amid a hundred petty and depressing cares, had not cramped her spiritual growth, and narrowed the sphere of her thought. Or was she still the same, and was it only he who had changed? At last he gave utterance to his wonder, and she answered him in those grave, earnest tones which seemed in themselves to be half a refutation of his doubts.

"It was easy for me to give you daring advice, then, Ralph," she said. "Like most school-girls, I thought that life was a great and glorious thing, and that happiness was a fruit which hung within reach of every hand. Now I have lived for six years trying single-handed to relieve the want and suffering of the needy people with whom I come in contact, and their squalor and wretchedness have sickened me, and, what is still worse, I feel that all I can do is as a drop in the ocean, and after all, amounts to nothing. I know I am no longer the same reckless girl, who, with the very best intention, sent you wandering through the wide world; and I thank God that it proved to be for your good, although the whole now appears quite incredible to me. My thoughts have moved so long within the narrow circle of these mountains that they have lost their youthful elasticity, and can no more rise above them."

Ralph detected, in the midst of her despondency, a spark of her former fire, and grew eloquent in his endeavors to persuade her that she was unjust to herself, and that there was but a wider sphere of life needed to develop all the latent powers of her rich nature.

At the dinner-table, her father again sat eyeing his guest with that same cold look of distrust and suspicion. And when the meal was at an end, he rose abruptly and called his daughter into another room. Presently Ralph heard his angry voice resounding through the house, interrupted now and then by a woman's sobs, and a subdued, passionate pleading. When Bertha again entered the room, her eyes were very red, and he saw that she had been weeping. She threw a shawl over her shoulders, beckoned to him with her hand, and he arose and followed her. She led the way silently until they reached a thick copse of birch and alder near the strand. She dropped down upon a bench between two trees, and he took his seat at her side.

"Ralph," began she, with a visible effort, "I hardly know what to say to you; but there is something which I must tell you--my father wishes you to leave us at once."

"And YOU, Bertha?"

"Well--yes--I wish it too."

She saw the painful shock which her words gave him, and she strove hard to speak. Her lips trembled, her eyes became suffused with tears, which grew and grew, but never fell; she could not utter a word.

"Well, Bertha," answered he, with a little quiver in his voice, "if you, too, wish me to go, I shall not tarry. Good-bye."

He rose quickly, and, with averted face, held out his hand to her; but as she made no motion to grasp the hand, he began distractedly to button his coat, and moved slowly away.

"Ralph."

He turned sharply, and, before he knew it, she lay sobbing upon his breast.

"Ralph," she murmured, while the tears almost choked her words, "I could not have you leave me thus. It is hard enough--it is hard enough--"

"What is hard, beloved?"

She raised her head abruptly, and turned upon him a gaze full of hope and doubt, and sweet perplexity.

"Ah, no, you do not love me," she whispered, sadly.

"Why should I come to seek you, after these many years, dearest, if I did not wish to make you my wife before God and men? Why should I--"

"Ah, yes, I know," she interrupted him with a fresh fit of weeping, "you are too good and honest to wish to throw me away, now when you have seen how my soul has hungered for the sight of you these many years, how even now I cling to you with a despairing clutch. But you cannot disguise yourself, Ralph, and I saw from the first moment that you loved me no more."

"Do not be such an unreasonable child," he remonstrated, feebly. "I do not love you with the wild, irrational passion of former years; but I have the tenderest regard for you, and my heart warms at the sight of your sweet face, and I shall do all in my power to make you as happy as any man can make you who--"

"Who does not love me," she finished.

A sudden shudder seemed to shake her whole frame, and she drew herself more tightly up to him.

"Ah, no," she continued, after a while, sinking back upon her seat. "It is a hopeless thing to compel a reluctant heart. I will accept no sacrifice from you. You owe me nothing, for you have acted toward me honestly and uprightly, and I shall be a stronger, or--at least--a better woman for what you gave me--and--for what you could not give me, even though you would."

"But, Bertha," exclaimed he, looking mournfully at her, "it is not true when you say that I owe you nothing. Six years ago, when first I wooed you, you could not return my love, and you sent me out into the world, and even refused to accept any pledge or promise for the future."

"And you returned," she responded, "a man, such as my hope had pictured you; but, while I had almost been standing still, you had outgrown me, and outgrown your old self, and, with your old self, outgrown its love for me, for your love was not of your new self, but of the old. Alas! it is a sad tale, but it is true."

She spoke gravely now, and with a steadier voice, but her eyes hung upon his face with an eager look of expectation, as if yearning to detect there some gleam of hope, some contradiction of the dismal truth. He read that look aright, and it pierced him like a sharp sword. He made a brave effort to respond to its appeal, but his features seemed hard as stone, and he could only cry out against his destiny, and bewail his misfortune and hers.

Toward evening, Ralph was sitting in an open boat, listening to the measured oar-strokes of the boatmen who were rowing him out to the nearest stopping-place of the steamer. The mountains lifted their great placid heads up among the sun-bathed clouds, and the fjord opened its cool depths as if to make room for their vast reflections. Ralph felt as if he were floating in the midst of the blue infinite space, and, with the strength which this feeling inspired, he tried to face boldly the thought from which he had but a moment ago shrunk as from something hopelessly sad and perplexing.

And in that hour he looked fearlessly into the gulf which separates the New World from the Old. He had hoped to bridge it; but, alas! it cannot be bridged.

A SCIENTIFIC VAGABOND.

I.

THE steamer which as far back as 1860 passed every week on its northward way up along the coast of Norway, was of a very sociable turn of mind. It ran with much shrieking and needless bluster in and out the calm, winding fjords, paid unceremonious little visits in every out-of-the-way nook and bay, dropped now and then a black heap of coal into the shining water, and sent thick volleys of smoke and shrill little echoes careering aimlessly among the mountains. It seemed, on the whole, from an aesthetic point of view, an objectionable phenomenon--a blot upon the perfect summer day. By the inhabitants, however, of these remote regions (with the exception of a few obstinate individuals, who had at first looked upon it as the sure herald of dooms-day, and still were vaguely wondering what the world was coming to,) it was regarded in a very different light. This choleric little monster was to them a friendly and welcome visitor, which established their connection with the outside world, and gave them a proud consciousness of living in the very heart of civilization. Therefore, on steamboat days they flocked en masse down on the piers, and, with an ever-fresh sense of novelty, greeted the approaching boat with lively cheers, with firing of muskets and waving of handkerchiefs. The men of condition, as the judge, the sheriff, and the parson, whose dignity forbade them to receive the steamer in person, contented themselves with watching it through an opera-glass from their balconies; and if a high official was known to be on board, they perhaps displayed the national banner from their flag-poles, as a delicate compliment to their superior.

But the Rev. Mr. Oddson, the parson of whom I have to speak, had this day yielded to the gentle urgings of his daughters (as, indeed, he always did), and had with them boarded the steamer to receive his nephew, Arnfinn Vording, who was returning from the university for his summer vacation. And now they had him between them in their pretty white-painted parsonage boat, with the blue line along the gunwale, beleaguering him with eager questions about friends and relatives in the capital, chums, university sports, and a medley of other things interesting to young ladies who have a collegian for a cousin. His uncle was charitable enough to check his own curiosity about the nephew's progress in the arts and sciences, and the result of his recent examinations, till he should have become fairly settled under his roof; and Arnfinn, who, in spite of his natural brightness and ready humor, was anything but a "dig," was grateful for the respite.

The parsonage lay snugly nestled at the end of the bay, shining contentedly through the green foliage from a multitude of small sun-smitten windows. Its pinkish whitewash, which was peeling off from long exposure to the weather, was in cheerful contrast to the broad black surface of the roof, with its glazed tiles, and the starlings' nests under the chimney-tops. The thick-leaved maples and walnut-trees which grew in random clusters about the walls seemed loftily conscious of standing there for purposes of protection; for, wherever their long-fingered branches happened to graze the roof, it was always with a touch, light, graceful, and airily caressing. The irregularly paved yard was inclosed on two sides by the main building, and on the third by a species of log cabin, which, in Norway, is called a brew-house; but toward the west the view was but slightly obscured by an elevated pigeon cot and a clump of birches, through whose sparse leaves the fjord beneath sent its rapid jets and gleams of light, and its strange suggestions of distance, peace and unaccountable gladness.

Arnfinn Vording's career had presented that subtle combination of farce and tragedy which most human lives are apt to be; and if the tragic element had during his early years been preponderating, he was hardly himself aware of it; for he had been too young at the death of his parents to feel that keenness of grief which the same privation would have given him at a later period of his life. It might have been humiliating to confess it, but it was nevertheless true that the terror he had once sustained on being pursued by a furious bull was much more vivid in his memory than the vague wonder and depression which had filled his mind at seeing his mother so suddenly stricken with age, as she lay motionless in her white robes in the front parlor. Since then his uncle, who was his guardian and nearest relative, had taken him into his family, had instructed him with his own daughters, and finally sent him to the University, leaving the little fortune which he had inherited to accumulate for future use. Arnfinn had a painfully distinct recollection of his early hardships in trying to acquire that soft pronunciation of the r which is peculiar to the western fjord districts of Norway, and which he admired so much in his cousins; for the merry-eyed Inga, who was less scrupulous by a good deal than her older sister, Augusta, had from the beginning persisted in interpreting their relation of cousinship as an unbounded privilege on her part to ridicule him for his personal peculiarities, and especially for his harsh r and his broad eastern accent. Her ridicule was always very good-natured, to be sure, but therefore no less annoying.

But--such is the perverseness of human nature--in spite of a series of apparent rebuffs, interrupted now and then by fits of violent attachment, Arnfinn had early selected this dimpled and yellow-haired young girl, with her piquant little nose, for his favorite cousin. It was the prospect of seeing her which, above all else, had lent, in anticipation, an altogether new radiance to the day when he should present himself in his home with the long-tasseled student cap on his head, the unnecessary "pinchers" on his nose, and with the other traditional paraphernalia of the Norwegian student. That great day had now come; Arnfinn sat at Inga's side playing with her white fingers, which lay resting on his knee, and covering the depth of his feeling with harmless banter about her "amusingly unclassical little nose." He had once detected her, when a child, standing before a mirror, and pinching this unhappy feature in the middle, in the hope of making it "like Augusta's;" and since then he had no longer felt so utterly defenseless whenever his own foibles were attacked.

"But what of your friend, Arnfinn?" exclaimed Inga, as she ran up the stairs of the pier. "He of whom you have written so much. I have been busy all the morning making the blue guest-chamber ready for him."

"Please, cousin," answered the student, in a tone of mock entreaty, "only an hour's respite! If we are to talk about Strand we must make a day of it, you know. And just now it seems so grand to be at home, and with you, that I would rather not admit even so genial a subject as Strand to share my selfish happiness."

"Ah, yes, you are right. Happiness is too often selfish. But tell me only why he didn't come and I'll release you."

"He IS coming."

"Ah! And when?"

"That I don't know. He preferred to take the journey on foot, and he may be here at almost any time. But, as I have told you, he is very uncertain. If he should happen to make the acquaintance of some interesting snipe, or crane, or plover, he may prefer its company to ours, and then there is no counting on him any longer. He may be as likely to turn up at the North Pole as at the Gran Parsonage."

"How very singular. You don't know how curious I am to see him."

And Inga walked on in silence under the sunny birches which grew along the road, trying vainly to picture to herself this strange phenomenon of a man.

"I brought his book," remarked Arnfinn, making a gigantic effort to be generous, for he felt dim stirrings of jealousy within him. "If you care to read it, I think it will explain him to you better than anything I could say."

II.

The Oddsons were certainly a happy family though not by any means a harmonious one. The excellent pastor, who was himself neutrally good, orthodox, and kind-hearted, had often, in the privacy of his own thought, wondered what hidden ancestral influences there might have been at work in giving a man so peaceable and inoffensive as himself two daughters of such strongly defined individuality. There was Augusta, the elder, who was what Arnfinn called "indiscriminately reformatory," and had a universal desire to improve everything, from the Government down to agricultural implements and preserve jars. As long as she was content to expend the surplus energy, which seemed to accumulate within her through the long eventless winters, upon the Zulu Mission, and other legitimate objects, the pastor thought it all harmless enough; although, to be sure, her enthusiasm for those naked and howling savages did at times strike him as being somewhat extravagant. But when occasionally, in her own innocent way, she put both his patience and his orthodoxy to the test by her exceedingly puzzling questions, then he could not, in the depth of his heart, restrain the wish that she might have been more like other young girls, and less ardently solicitous about the fate of her kind. Affectionate and indulgent, however, as the pastor was, he would often, in the next moment, do penance for his unregenerate thought, and thank God for having made her so fair to behold, so pure, and so noble-hearted.

Toward Arnfinn, Augusta had, although of his own age, early assumed a kind of elder-sisterly relation; she had been his comforter during all the trials of his boy-hood; had yielded him her sympathy with that eager impulse which lay so deep in her nature, and had felt forlorn when life had called him away to where her words of comfort could not reach him. But when once she had hinted this to her father, he had pedantically convinced her that her feeling was unchristian, and Inga had playfully remarked that the hope that some one might soon find the open Polar Sea would go far toward consoling her for her loss; for Augusta had glorious visions at that time of the open Polar Sea. Now, the Polar Sea, and many other things, far nearer and dearer, had been forced into uneasy forgetfulness; and Arnfinn was once more with her, no longer a child, and no longer appealing to her for aid and sympathy; man enough, apparently, to have outgrown his boyish needs and still boy enough to be ashamed of having ever had them.

It was the third Sunday after Arnfinn's return. He and Augusta were climbing the hillside to the "Giant's Hood," from whence they had a wide view of the fjord, and could see the sun trailing its long bridge of flame upon the water. It was Inga's week in the kitchen, therefore her sister was Arnfinn's companion. As they reached the crest of the "Hood," Augusta seated herself on a flat bowlder, and the young student flung himself on a patch of greensward at her feet. The intense light of the late sun fell upon the girl's unconscious face, and Arnfinn lay, gazing up into it, and wondering at its rare beauty; but he saw only the clean cut of its features and the purity of its form, being too shallow to recognize the strong and heroic soul which had struggled so long for utterance in the life of which he had been a blind and unmindful witness.

"Gracious, how beautiful you are, cousin!" he broke forth, heedlessly, striking his leg with his slender cane; "pity you were not born a queen; you would be equal to almost anything, even if it were to discover the Polar Sea."

"I thought you were looking at the sun, Arnfinn," answered she, smiling reluctantly.

"And so I am, cousin," laughed he, with an other-emphatic slap of his boot.

"That compliment is rather stale."

"But the opportunity was too tempting."

"Never mind, I will excuse you from further efforts. Turn around and notice that wonderful purple halo which is hovering over the forests below. Isn't it glorious?"

"No, don't let us be solemn, pray. The sun I have seen a thousand times before, but you I have seen very seldom of late. Somehow, since I returned this time, you seem to keep me at a distance. You no longer confide to me your great plans for the abolishment of war, and the improvement of mankind generally. Why don't you tell me whether you have as yet succeeded in convincing the peasants that cleanliness is a cardinal virtue, that hawthorn hedges are more picturesque than rail fences, and that salt meat is a very indigestible article?"

"You know the fate of my reforms, from long experience," she answered, with the same sad, sweet smile. "I am afraid there must be some thing radically wrong about my methods; and, moreover, I know that your aspirations and mine are no longer the same, if they ever have been, and I am not ungenerous enough to force you to feign an interest which you do not feel."

"Yes, I know you think me flippant and boyish," retorted he, with sudden energy, and tossing a stone down into the gulf below. "But, by the way, my friend Strand, if he ever comes, would be just the man for you. He has quite as many hobbies as you have, and, what is more, he has a profound respect for hobbies in general, and is universally charitable toward those of others."

"Your friend is a great man," said the girl, earnestly. "I have read his book on `The Wading Birds of the Norwegian Highlands,' and none but a great man could have written it."

"He is an odd stick, but, for all that, a capital fellow; and I have no doubt you would get on admirably with him."

At this moment the conversation was interrupted by the appearance of the pastor's man, Hans, who came to tell the "young miss" that there was a big tramp hovering about the barns in the "out-fields," where he had been sleeping during the last three nights. He was a dangerous character, Hans thought, at least judging from his looks, and it was hardly safe for the young miss to be roaming about the fields at night as long as he was in the neighborhood.

"Why don't you speak to the pastor, and have him arrested?" said Arnfinn, impatient of Hans's long-winded recital.

"No, no, say nothing to father," demanded Augusta, eagerly. "Why should you arrest a poor man as long as he does nothing worse than sleep in the barns in the out-fields?"

"As you say, miss," retorted Hans, and departed.

The moon came up pale and mist-like over the eastern mountain ridges, struggled for a few brief moments feebly with the sunlight, and then vanished.

"It is strange," said Arnfinn, "how everything reminds me of Strand to-night. What gloriously absurd apostrophes to the moon he could make! I have not told you, cousin, of a very singular gift which he possesses. He can attract all kinds of birds and wild animals to himself; he can imitate their voices, and they flock around him, as if he were one of them, without fear of harm."

"How delightful," cried Augusta, with sudden animation. "What a glorious man your friend must be!"

"Because the snipes and the wild ducks like him? You seem to have greater confidence in their judgment than in mine."

"Of course I have--at least as long as you persist in joking. But, jesting aside, what a wondrously beautiful life he must lead whom Nature takes thus into her confidence; who has, as it were, an inner and subtler sense, corresponding to each grosser and external one; who is keen-sighted enough to read the character of every individual beast, and has ears sensitive to the full pathos of joy or sorrow in the song of the birds that inhabit our woodlands."

"Whether he has any such second set of senses as you speak of, I don't know; but there can be no doubt that his familiarity, not to say intimacy, with birds and beasts gives him a great advantage as a naturalist. I suppose you know that his little book has been translated into French, and rewarded with the gold medal of the Academy."

"Hush! What is that?" Augusta sprang up, and held her hand to her ear.

"Some love-lorn mountain-cock playing yonder in the pine copse," suggested Arnfinn, amused at his cousin's eagerness.

"You silly boy! Don't you know the mountain-cock never plays except at sunrise?"

"He would have a sorry time of it now, then, when there IS no sunrise."

"And so he has; he does not play except in early spring."

The noise, at first faint, now grew louder. It began with a series of mellow, plaintive clucks that followed thickly one upon another, like smooth pearls of sound that rolled through the throat in a continuous current; then came a few sharp notes as of a large bird that snaps his bill; then a long, half-melodious rumbling, intermingled with cacklings and snaps, and at last, a sort of diminuendo movement of the same round, pearly clucks. There was a whizzing of wing-beats in the air; two large birds swept over their heads and struck down into the copse whence the sound had issued.

"This is indeed a most singular thing," said Augusta, under her breath, and with wide-eyed wonder. "Let us go nearer, and see what it can be."

"I am sure I can go if you can," responded Arnfinn, not any too eagerly. "Give me your hand, and we can climb the better."

As they approached the pine copse, which projected like a promontory from the line of the denser forest, the noise ceased, and only the plaintive whistling of a mountain-hen, calling her scattered young together, and now and then the shrill response of a snipe to the cry of its lonely mate, fell upon the summer night, not as an interruption, but as an outgrowth of the very silence. Augusta stole with soundless tread through the transparent gloom which lingered under those huge black crowns, and Arnfinn followed impatiently after. Suddenly she motioned to him to stand still, and herself bent forward in an attitude of surprise and eager observation. On the ground, some fifty steps from where she was stationed, she saw a man stretched out full length, with a knapsack under his head, and surrounded by a flock of downy, half-grown birds, which responded with a low, anxious piping to his alluring cluck, then scattered with sudden alarm, only to return again in the same curious, cautious fashion as before. Now and then there was a great flapping of wings in the trees overhead, and a heavy brown and black speckled mountain-hen alighted close to the man's head, stretched out her neck toward him, cocked her head, called her scattered brood together, and departed with slow and deliberate wing-beats.

Again there was a frightened flutter overhead, a shrill anxious whistle rose in the air, and all was silence. Augusta had stepped on a dry branch--it had broken under her weight--hence the sudden confusion and flight. The unknown man had sprung up, and his eye, after a moment's search, had found the dark, beautiful face peering forth behind the red fir-trunk. He did not speak or salute her; he greeted her with silent joy, as one greets a wondrous vision which is too frail and bright for consciousness to grasp, which is lost the very instant one is conscious of seeing. But, while to the girl the sight, as it were, hung trembling in the range of mere physical perception, while its suddenness held it aloof from moral reflection, there came a great shout from behind, and Arnfinn, whom in her surprise she had quite forgotten, came bounding forward, grasping the stranger by the hand with much vigor, laughing heartily, and pouring forth a confused stream of delighted interjections, borrowed from all manner of classical and unclassical tongues.

"Strand! Strand!" he cried, when the first tumult of excitement had subsided; "you most marvelous and incomprehensible Strand! From what region of heaven or earth did you jump down into our prosaic neighborhood? And what in the world possessed you to choose our barns as the centre of your operations, and nearly put me to the necessity of having you arrested for vagrancy? How I do regret that Cousin Augusta's entreaties mollified my heart toward you. Pardon me, I have not introduced you. This is my cousin, Miss Oddson, and this is my miraculous friend, the world-renowned author, vagrant, and naturalist, Mr. Marcus Strand."

Strand stepped forward, made a deep but somewhat awkward bow, and was dimly aware that a small soft hand was extended to him, and, in the next moment, was enclosed in his own broad and voluminous palm. He grasped it firmly, and, in one of those profound abstractions into which he was apt to fall when under the sway of a strong impression, pressed it with increasing cordiality, while he endeavored to find fitting answers to Arnfinn's multifarious questions.

"To tell the truth, Vording," he said, in a deep, full-ringing bass, "I didn't know that these were your cousin's barns--I mean that your uncle"--giving the unhappy hand an emphatic shake--"inhabited these barns."

"No, thank heaven, we are not quite reduced to that," cried Arnfinn, gayly; "we still boast a parsonage, as you will presently discover, and a very bright and cozy one, to boot. But, whatever you do, have the goodness to release Augusta's hand. Don't you see how desperately she is struggling, poor thing?"

Strand dropped the hand as if it had been a hot coal, blushed to the edge of his hair, and made another profound reverence. He was a tall, huge-limbed youth, with a frame of gigantic mold, and a large, blonde, shaggy head, like that of some good-natured antediluvian animal, which might feel the disadvantages of its size amid the puny beings of this later stage of creation. There was a frank directness in his gaze, and an unconsciousness of self, which made him very winning, and which could not fail of its effect upon a girl who, like Augusta, was fond of the uncommon, and hated smooth, facile and well-tailored young men, with the labels of society and fashion upon their coats, their mustaches, and their speech. And Strand, with his large sun-burned face, his wild-growing beard, blue woolen shirt, top boots, and unkempt appearance generally, was a sufficiently startling phenomenon to satisfy even so exacting a fancy as hers; for, after reading his book about the Wading Birds, she had made up her mind that he must have few points of resemblance to the men who had hitherto formed part of her own small world, although she had not until now decided just in what way he was to differ.

"Suppose I help you carry your knapsack," said Arnfinn, who was flitting about like a small nimble spaniel trying to make friends with some large, good-natured Newfoundland. "You must be very tired, having roamed about in this Quixotic fashion!"

"No, I thank you," responded Strand, with an incredulous laugh, glancing alternately from Arnfinn to the knapsack, as if estimating their proportionate weight. "I am afraid you would rue your bargain if I accepted it."

"I suppose you have a great many stuffed birds at home," remarked the girl, looking with self-forgetful admiration at the large brawny figure.

"No, I have hardly any," answered he, seating himself on the ground, and pulling a thick note-book from his pocket. "I prefer live creatures. Their anatomical and physiological peculiarities have been studied by others, and volumes have been written about them. It is their psychological traits, ii you will allow the expression, which interest me, and those I can only get at while they are alive."

"How delightful!"

Some minutes later they were all on their way to the Parsonage. The sun, in spite of its mid-summer wakefulness, was getting red-eyed and drowsy, and the purple mists which hung in scattered fragments upon the forest below had lost something of their deep-tinged brilliancy. But Augusta, quite blind to the weakened light effects, looked out upon the broad landscape in ecstasy, and, appealing to her more apathetic companions, invited them to share her joy at the beauty of the faint-flushed summer night.

"You are getting quite dithyrambic, my dear," remarked Arnfinn, with an air of cousinly superiority, which he felt was eminently becoming to him; and Augusta looked up with quick surprise, then smiled in an absent way, and forgot what she had been saying. She had no suspicion but that her enthusiasm had been all for the sunset.

III.

In a life so outwardly barren and monotonous as Augusta's--a life in which the small external events were so firmly interwoven with the subtler threads of yearnings, wants, and desires--the introduction of so large and novel a fact as Marcus Strand would naturally produce some perceptible result. It was that deplorable inward restlessness of hers, she reasoned, which had hitherto made her existence seem so empty and unsatisfactory; but now his presence filled the hours, and the newness of his words, his manner, and his whole person afforded inexhaustible material for thought. It was now a week since his arrival, and while Arnfinn and Inga chatted at leisure, drew caricatures, or read aloud to each other in some shady nook of the garden, she and Strand would roam along the beach, filling the vast unclouded horizon with large glowing images of the future of the human race. He always listened in sympathetic silence while she unfolded to him her often childishly daring schemes for the amelioration of suffering and the righting of social wrongs; and when she had finished, and he met the earnest appeal of her dark eye, there would often be a pause, during which each, with a half unconscious lapse from the impersonal, would feel more keenly the joy of this new and delicious mental companionship. And when at length he answered, sometimes gently refuting and sometimes assenting to her proposition, it was always with a slow, deliberate earnestness, as if he felt but her deep sincerity, and forgot for the moment her sex, her youth, and her inexperience. It was just this kind of fellowship for which she had hungered so long, and her heart went out with a great gratitude toward this strong and generous man, who was willing to recognize her humanity, and to respond with an ever-ready frankness, unmixed with petty suspicions and second thoughts, to the eager needs of her half-starved nature. It is quite characteristic, too, of the type of womanhood which Augusta represents (and with which this broad continent of ours abounds), that, with her habitual disregard of appearances, she would have scorned the notion that their intercourse had any ultimate end beyond that of mutual pleasure and instruction.

It was early in the morning in the third week of Strand's stay at the Parsonage. A heavy dew had fallen during the night, and each tiny grass-blade glistened in the sun, bending under the weight of its liquid diamond. The birds were improvising a miniature symphony in the birches at the end of the garden; the song-thrush warbled with a sweet melancholy his long-drawn contralto notes; the lark, like a prima donna, hovering conspicuously in mid air, poured forth her joyous soprano solo; and the robin, quite unmindful of the tempo, filled out the pauses with his thoughtless staccato chirp. Augusta, who was herself the early bird of the pastor's family, had paid a visit to the little bath-house down at the brook, and was now hurrying homeward, her heavy black hair confined in a delicate muslin hood, and her lithe form hastily wrapped in a loose morning gown. She had paused for a moment under the birches to listen to the song of the lark, when suddenly a low, half articulate sound, very unlike the voice of a bird, arrested her attention; she raised her eyes, and saw Strand sitting in the top of a tree, apparently conversing with himself, or with some tiny thing which he held in his hands.

"Ah, yes, you poor little sickly thing!" she heard him mutter. "Don't you make such an ado now. You shall soon be quite well, if you will only mind what I tell you. Stop, stop! Take it easy. It is all for your own good, you know. If you had only been prudent, and not stepped on your lame leg, you might have been spared this affliction. But, after all, it was not your fault--it was that foolish little mother of yours. She will remember now that a skein of hemp thread is not the thing to line her nest with. If she doesn't, you may tell her that it was I who said so."

Augusta stood gazing on in mute astonishment; then, suddenly remembering her hasty toilet, she started to run; but, as chance would have it, a dry branch, which hung rather low, caught at her hood, and her hair fell in a black wavy stream down over her shoulders. She gave a little cry, the tree shook violently, and Strand was at her side. She blushed crimson over neck and face, and, in her utter bewilderment, stood like a culprit before him, unable to move, unable to speak, and only returning with a silent bow his cordial greeting. It seemed to her that she had ungenerously intruded upon his privacy, watching him, while he thought himself unobserved. And Augusta was quite unskilled in those social accomplishments which enable young ladies to hide their inward emotions under a show of polite indifference, for, however hard she strove, she could not suppress a slight quivering of her lips, and her intense self-reproach made Strand's words fall dimly on her ears, and prevented her from gathering the meaning of what he was saying. He held in his hands a young bird with a yellow line along the edge of its bill (and there was something beautifully soft and tender in the way those large palms of his handled any living thing), and he looked pityingly at it while he spoke.

"The mother of this little linnet," he said, smiling, "did what many foolish young mothers are apt to do. She took upon her the responsibility of raising offspring without having acquired the necessary knowledge of housekeeping. So she lined her nest with hemp, and the consequence was, that her first-born got his legs entangled, and was obliged to remain in the nest long after his wings had reached their full development. I saw her feeding him about a week ago, and, as my curiosity prompted me to look into the case, I released the little cripple, cleansed the deep wound which the threads had cut in his flesh, and have since been watching him during his convalescence. Now he is quite in a fair way, but I had to apply some salve, and to cut off the feathers about the wound, and the little fool squirmed under the pain, and grew rebellious. Only notice this scar, if you please, Miss Oddson, and you may imagine what the poor thing must have suffered."

Augusta gave a start; she timidly raised her eyes, and saw Strand's grave gaze fixed upon her. She felt as if some intolerable spell had come over her, and, as her agitation increased, her power of speech seemed utterly to desert her.

"Ah, you have not been listening to me?" said Strand, in a tone of wondering inquiry. "Pardon me for presuming to believe that my little invalid could be as interesting to you as he is to me."

"Mr. Strand," stammered the girl, while the invisible tears came near choking her voice. "Mr. Strand--I didn't mean--really--"

She knew that if she said another word she should burst into tears. With a violent effort, she gathered up her wrapper, which somehow had got unbuttoned at the neck, and, with heedlessly hurrying steps, darted away toward the house.

Strand stood looking after her, quite unmindful of his feathered patient, which flew chirping about him in the grass. Two hours later Arnfinn found him sitting under the birches with his hands clasped over the top of his head, and his surgical instruments scattered on the ground around him.

"Corpo di Baccho," exclaimed the student, stooping to pick up the precious tools; "have you been amputating your own head, or is it I who am dreaming?"

"Ah," murmured Strand, lifting a large, strange gaze upon his friend, "is it you?"

"Who else should it be? I come to call you to breakfast."

IV.

"I wonder what is up between Strand and Augusta?" said Arnfinn to his cousin Inga. The questioner was lying in the grass at her feet, resting his chin on his palms, and gazing with roguishly tender eyes up into her fresh, blooming face; but Inga, who was reading aloud from "David Copperfield," and was deep in the matrimonial tribulations of that noble hero, only said "hush," and continued reading. Arnfinn, after a minute's silence, repeated his remark, whereupon his fair cousin wrenched his cane out of his hand, and held it threateningly over his head.

"Will you be a good boy and listen?" she exclaimed, playfully emphasizing each word with a light rap on his curly pate.

"Ouch! that hurts," cried Arnfinn, and dodged.

"It was meant to hurt," replied Inga, with mock severity, and returned to "Copperfield."

Presently the seed of a corn-flower struck the tip of her nose, and again the cane was lifted; but Dora's housekeeping experiences were too absorbingly interesting, and the blue eyes could not resist their fascination.

"Cousin Inga," said Arnfinn, and this time with as near an approach to earnestness as he was capable of at that moment, "I do believe that Strand is in love with Augusta."

Inga dropped the book, and sent him what was meant to be a glance of severe rebuke, and then said, in her own amusingly emphatic way:

"I do wish you wouldn't joke with such things, Arnfinn."

"Joke! Indeed I am not joking. I wish to heaven that I were. What a pity it is that she has taken such a dislike to him!"

"Dislike! Oh, you are a profound philosopher, you are! You think that because she avoids--"

Here Inga abruptly clapped her hand over her mouth, and, with sudden change of voice and expression, said:

"I am as silent as the grave."

"Yes, you are wonderfully discreet," cried Arnfinn, laughing, while the girl bit her under lip with an air of penitence and mortification which, in any other bosom than a cousin's would have aroused compassion.

"Aha! So steht's!" he broke forth, with another burst of merriment; then, softened by the sight of a tear that was slowly gathering beneath her eyelashes, he checked his laughter, crept up to her side, and in a half childishly coaxing, half caressing tone, he whispered:

"Dear little cousin, indeed I didn't mean to hurt your feelings. You are not angry with me, are you? And if you will only promise me not to tell, I have something here which I should like to show you."

He well knew that there was nothing which would sooner soothe Inga's wrath than confiding a secret to her; and while he was a boy, he had, in cases of sore need, invented secrets lest his life should be made miserable by the sense that she was displeased with him. In this instance her anger was not strong enough to resist the anticipation of a secret, probably relating to that little drama which had, during the last weeks, been in progress under her very eyes. With a resolute movement, she brushed her tears away, bent eagerly forward, and, in the next moment, her face was all expectancy and animation.

Arnfinn pulled a thick black note-book from his breast pocket, opened it in his lap, and read:

"August 3, 5 A. M.--My little invalid is doing finely; he seemed to relish much a few dozen flies which I brought him in my hand. His pulse is to-day, for the first time, normal. He is beginning to step on the injured leg without apparent pain.

"10 A. M.--Miss Augusta's eyes have a strange, lustrous brilliancy whenever she speaks of subjects which seem to agitate the depths of her being. How and why is it that an excessive amount of feeling always finds its first expression in the eye? One kind of emotion seems to widen the pupil, another kind to contract it. TO be noticed in future, how particular emotions affect the eye.

"6 P. M.--I met a plover on the beach this afternoon. By imitating his cry, I induced him to come within a few feet of me. The plover, as his cry indicates, is a very melancholy bird. In fact I believe the melancholy temperament to be prevailing among the wading birds, as the phlegmatic among birds of prey. The singing birds are choleric or sanguine. Tease a thrush, or even a lark, and you will soon be convinced. A snipe, or plover, as far as my experience goes, seldom shows anger; you cannot tease them. To be considered, how far the voice of a bird may be indicative of its temperament.

"August 5, 9 P. M.--Since the unfortunate meeting yesterday morning, when my intense pre-occupation with my linnet, which had torn its wound open again, probably made me commit some breach of etiquette, Miss Augusta avoids me.

"August 7--I am in a most singular state. My pulse beats 85, which is a most unheard-of thing for me, as my pulse is naturally full and slow. And, strangely enough, I do not feel at all unwell. On the contrary, my physical well-being is rather heightened than otherwise. The life of a whole week is crowded into a day, and that of a day into an hour."

Inga, who, at several points of this narrative, had been struggling hard to preserve her gravity, here burst into a ringing laugh.

"That is what I call scientific love-making," said Arnfinn, looking up from the book with an expression of subdued amusement.

"But Arnfinn," cried the girl, while the laughter quickly died out of her face, "does Mr. Strand know that you are reading this?"

"To be sure he does. And that is just what to my mind makes the situation so excessively comical. He has himself no suspicion that this book contains anything but scientific notes. He appears to prefer the empiric method in love as in philosophy. I verily believe that he is innocently experimenting with himself, with a view to making some great physiological discovery."

"And so he will, perhaps," rejoined the girl, the mixture of gayety and grave solicitude making her face, as her cousin thought, particularly charming.

"Only not a physiological, but possibly a psychological one," remarked Arnfinn. "But listen to this. Here is something rich:

"August 9--Miss Augusta once said something about the possibility of animals being immortal. Her eyes shone with a beautiful animation as she spoke. I am longing to continue the subject with her. It haunts me the whole day long. There may be more in the idea than appears to a superficial observer."

"Oh, how charmingly he understands how to deceive himself," cried Inga.

"Merely a quid pro quo," said Arnfinn.

"I know what I shall do!"

"And so do I."

"Won't you tell me, please?"

"No."

"Then I sha'n't tell you either."

And they flew apart like two thoughtless little birds ("sanguine," as Strand would have called them), each to ponder on some formidable plot for the reconciliation of the estranged lovers.

V.

During the week that ensued, the multifarious sub-currents of Strand's passion seemed slowly to gather themselves into one clearly defined stream, and, after much scientific speculation, he came to the conclusion that he loved Augusta. In a moment of extreme discouragement, he made a clean breast of it to Arnfinn, at the same time informing him that he had packed his knapsack, and would start on his wanderings again the next morning. All his friend's entreaties were in vain; he would and must go. Strand was an exasperatingly headstrong fellow, and persuasions never prevailed with him. He had confirmed himself in the belief that he was very unattractive to women, and that Augusta, of all women, for some reason which was not quite clear to him, hated and abhorred him. Inexperienced as he was, he could see no reason why she should avoid him, if she did not hate him. They sat talking until midnight, each entangling himself in those passionate paradoxes and contradictions peculiar to passionate and impulsive youth. Strand paced the floor with large steps, pouring out his long pent-up emotion in violent tirades of self-accusation and regret; while Arnfinn sat on the bed, trying to soothe his excitement by assuring him that he was not such a monster as, for the moment, he had believed himself to be, but only succeeding, in spite of all his efforts, in pouring oil on the flames. Strand was scientifically convinced that Nature, in accordance with some inscrutable law of equilibrium, had found it necessary to make him physically unattractive, perhaps to indemnify mankind for that excess of intellectual gifts which, at the expense of the race at large, she had bestowed upon him.

Early the next morning, as a kind of etherealized sunshine broke through the white muslin curtains of Arnfinn's room, and long streaks of sun-illumined dust stole through the air toward the sleeper's pillow, there was a sharp rap at the door, and Strand entered. His knapsack was strapped over his shoulders, his long staff was in his hand, and there was an expression of conscious martyrdom in his features. Arnfinn raised himself on his elbows, and rubbed his eyes with a desperate determination to get awake, but only succeeded in gaining a very dim impression of a beard, a blue woolen shirt, and a disproportionately large shoe buckle. The figure advanced to the bed, extended a broad, sun-burned hand, and a deep bass voice was heard to say:

"Good-bye, brother."

Arnfinn, who was a hard sleeper, gave another rub, and, in a querulously sleepy tone, managed to mutter:

"Why,--is it as late as that--already?"

The words of parting were more remotely repeated, the hand closed about Arnfinn's half-unfeeling fingers, the lock on the door gave a little sharp click, and all was still. But the sunshine drove the dust in a dumb, confused dance through the room.

Some four hours later, Arnfinn woke up with a vague feeling as if some great calamity had happened; he was not sure but that he had slept a fortnight or more. He dressed with a sleepy, reckless haste, being but dimly conscious of the logic of the various processes of ablution which he underwent. He hurried up to Strand's room, but, as he had expected, found it empty.

During all the afternoon, the reading of "David Copperfield" was interrupted by frequent mutual condolences, and at times Inga's hand would steal up to her eye to brush away a treacherous tear. But then she only read the faster, and David and Agnes were already safe in the haven of matrimony before either she or Arnfinn was aware that they had struggled successfully through the perilous reefs and quicksands of courtship.

Augusta excused herself from supper, Inga's forced devices at merriment were too transparent, Arnfinn's table-talk was of a rambling, incoherent sort, and he answered dreadfully malapropos, if a chance word was addressed to him, and even the good-natured pastor began, at last, to grumble; for the inmates of the Gran Parsonage seemed to have but one life and one soul in common, and any individual disturbance immediately disturbed the peace and happiness of the whole household. Now gloom had, in some unaccountable fashion, obscured the common atmosphere. Inga shook her small wise head, and tried to extract some little consolation from the consciousness that she knew at least some things which Arnfinn did not know, and which it would be very unsafe to confide to him.

VI.

Four weeks after Strand's departure, as the summer had already assumed that tinge of sadness which impresses one as a foreboding of coming death, Augusta was walking along the beach, watching the flight of the sea-birds. Her latest "aberration," as Arnfinn called it, was an extraordinary interest in the habits of the eider-ducks, auks, and sea-gulls, the noisy monotony of whose existence had, but a few months ago, appeared to her the symbol of all that was vulgar and coarse in human and animal life. Now she had even provided herself with a note-book, and (to use once more the language of her unbelieving cousin) affected a half-scientific interest in their clamorous pursuits. She had made many vain attempts to imitate their voices and to beguile them into closer intimacy, and had found it hard at times to suppress her indignation when they persisted in viewing her in the light of an intruder, and in returning her amiable approaches with shy suspicion, as if they doubted the sincerity of her intentions.

She was a little paler now, perhaps, than before, but her eyes had still the same lustrous depth, and the same sweet serenity was still diffused over her features, and softened, like a pervading tinge of warm color, the grand simplicity of her presence. She sat down on a large rock, picked up a curiously twisted shell, and seeing a plover wading in the surf, gave a soft, low whistle, which made the bird turn round and gaze at her with startled distrust. She repeated the call, but perhaps a little too eagerly, and the bird spread its wings with a frightened cry, and skimmed, half flying, half running, out over the glittering surface of the fjord. But from the rocks close by came a long melancholy whistle like that of a bird in distress, and the girl rose and hastened with eager steps toward the spot. She climbed up on a stone, fringed all around with green slimy seaweeds, in order to gain a wider view of the beach. Then suddenly some huge figure started up between the rocks at her feet; she gave a little scream, her foot slipped, and in the next moment she lay--in Strand's arms. He offered no apology, but silently carried her over the slippery stones, and deposited her tenderly upon the smooth white sand. There it occurred to her that his attention was quite needless, but at the moment she was too startled to make any remonstrance.

"But how in the world, Mr. Strand, did you come here?" she managed at last to stammer. "We all thought that you had gone away."

"I hardly know myself," said Strand, in a beseeching undertone, quite different from his usual confident bass. "I only know that--that I was very wretched, and that I had to come back."

Then there was a pause, which to both seemed quite interminable, and, in order to fill it out in some way, Strand began to move his head and arms uneasily, and at length seated himself at Augusta's side. The blood was beating with feverish vehemence in her temples, and for the first time in her life she felt something akin to pity for this large, strong man, whose strength and cheerful self-reliance had hitherto seemed to raise him above the need of a woman's aid and sympathy. Now the very shabbiness of his appearance, and the look of appealing misery in his features, opened in her bosom the gate through which compassion could enter, and, with that generous self-forgetfulness which was the chief factor of her character, she leaned over toward him, and said:

"You must have been very sick, Mr. Strand. Why did you not come to us and allow us to take care of you, instead of roaming about here in this stony wilderness?"

"Yes; I have been sick," cried Strand, with sudden vehemence, seizing her hand; "but it is a sickness of which I shall never, never be healed."

And with that world-old eloquence which is yet ever new, he poured forth his passionate confession in her ear, and she listened, hungrily at first, then with serene, wide-eyed happiness. He told her how, driven by his inward restlessness, he had wandered about in the mountains, until one evening at a saeter, he had heard a peasant lad singing a song, in which this stanza occurred:

"A woman's frown, a woman's smile,
Nor hate nor fondness prove;
For maidens smile on him they hate,
And fly from him they love."

Then it had occurred to him for the first time in his life that a woman's behavior need not be the logical indicator of her deepest feelings, and, enriched with this joyful discovery, inspired with new hope, he had returned, but had not dared at once to seek the Parsonage, until he could invent some plausible reason for his return; but his imagination was very poor, and he had found none, except that he loved the pastor's beautiful daughter.

The evening wore on. The broad mountain-guarded valley, flooded now to the brim with a soft misty light, spread out about them, and filled them with a delicious sense of security. The fjord lifted its grave gaze toward the sky, and deepened responsively with a bright, ever-receding immensity. The young girl felt this blessed peace gently stealing over her; doubt and struggle were all past, and the sun shone ever serene and unobscured upon the widening expanses of the future. And in his breast, too, that mood reigned in which life looks boundless and radiant, human woes small or impossible, and one's own self large and all-conquering. In that hour they remodeled this old and obstinate world of ours, never doubting that, if each united his faith and strength with the other's, they could together lift its burden.

That night was the happiest and most memorable night in the history of the Gran Parsonage. The pastor walked up and down on the floor, rubbing his hands in quiet contentment. Inga, to whom an engagement was essentially a solemn affair, sat in a corner and gazed at her sister and Strand with tearful radiance. Arnfinn gave vent to his joy by bestowing embraces promiscuously upon whomsoever chanced to come in his way.

This story, however, has a brief but not unimportant sequel. It was not many weeks after this happy evening that Arnfinn and the maiden with the "amusingly unclassical nose" presented themselves in the pastor's study and asked for his paternal and unofficial blessing. But the pastor, I am told, grew very wroth, and demanded that his nephew should first take his second and third degrees, attaching, besides, some very odious stipulations regarding average in study and college standing, before there could be any talk about engagement or matrimony. So, at present, Arnfinn is still studying, and the fair-haired Inga is still waiting.

TRULS, THE NAMELESS.

HE was born in the houseman's lodge; she in the great mansion. He did not know who his father was; she was the daughter of Grim of Skogli, and she was the only daughter he had. They were carried to baptism on the same day, and he was called Truls, because they had to call him something; she received the name of Borghild, because that had been the name of every eldest born daughter in the family for thirty generations. They both cried when the pastor poured the water on their heads; his mother hushed him, blushed, and looked timidly around her; but the woman who carried Borghild lifted her high up in her arms so that everybody could see her, and the pastor smiled benignly, and the parishioners said that they had never seen so beautiful a child. That was the way in which they began life--he as a child of sin, she as the daughter of a mighty race.

They grew up together. She had round cheeks and merry eyes, and her lips were redder than the red rose. He was of slender growth, his face was thin and pale, and his eyes had a strange, benumbed gaze, as if they were puzzling themselves with some sad, life-long riddle which they never hoped to solve. On the strand where they played the billows came and went, and they murmured faintly with a sound of infinite remoteness. Borghild laughed aloud, clapped her hands and threw stones out into the water, while he sat pale and silent, and saw the great white-winged sea-birds sailing through the blue ocean of the sky.

"How would you like to live down there in the deep green water?" she asked him one day, as they sat watching the eider-ducks which swam and dived, and stood on their heads among the sea-weeds.

"I should like it very well," he answered, "if you would follow me."

"No, I won't follow you," she cried. "It is cold and wet down in the water. And I should spoil the ribbons on my new bodice. But when I grow up and get big and can braid my hair, then I shall row with the young lads to the church yonder on the headland, and there the old pastor will marry me, and I shall wear the big silver crown which my mother wore when she was married."

"And may I go with you?" asked he, timidly.

"Yes, you may steer my boat and be my helmsman, or--you may be my bridegroom, if you would like that better."

"Yes, I think I should rather be your bridegroom," and he gave her a long, strange look which almost frightened her.

The years slipped by, and before Borghild knew it, she had grown into womanhood. The down on Truls's cheeks became rougher, and he, too, began to suspect that he was no longer a boy. When the sun was late and the breeze murmured in the great, dark-crowned pines, they often met by chance, at the well, on the strand, or on the saeter-green. And the oftener they met the more they found to talk about; to be sure, it was she who did the talking, and he looked at her with his large wondering eyes and listened. She told him of the lamb which had tumbled down over a steep precipice and still was unhurt, of the baby who pulled the pastor's hair last Sunday during the baptismal ceremony, or of the lumberman, Lars, who drank the kerosene his wife gave him for brandy, and never knew the difference. But, when the milkmaids passed by, she would suddenly forget what she had been saying, and then they sat gazing at each other in silence. Once she told him of the lads who danced with her at the party at Houg; and she thought she noticed a deeper color on his face, and that he clinched both his fists and--thrust them into his pockets. That set her thinking, and the more she thought, the more curious she grew. He played the violin well; suppose she should ask him to come and fiddle at the party her father was to give at the end of the harvest. She resolved to do it, and he, not knowing what moved her, gave his promise eagerly. It struck her, afterward, that she had done a wicked thing, but, like most girls, she had not the heart to wrestle with an uncomfortable thought; she shook it off and began to hum a snatch of an old song.

> "O'er the billows the fleet-footed storm-wind rode,
> The billows blue are the merman's abode,
> So strangely that harp was sounding."

The memory of old times came back to her, the memory of the morning long years ago, when they sat together on the strand, and he said; "I think I would rather be your bridegroom, Borghild." The memory was sweet but it was bitter too; and the bitterness rose and filled her heart. She threw her head back proudly, and laughed a strange, hollow laugh. "A bastard's bride, ha, ha! A fine tale were that for the parish gossips." A yellow butterfly lighted on her arm, and with a fierce frown on her face she caught it between her fingers. Then she looked pityingly on the dead wings, as they lay in her hand, and murmured between her teeth: "Poor thing! Why did you come in my way, unbidden?"

The harvest was rich, and the harvest party was to keep pace with the harvest. The broad Skogli mansion was festively lighted (for it was already late in September); the tall, straight tallow candles, stuck in many-armed candlesticks, shone dimly through a sort of misty halo, and only suffused the dusk with a faint glimmering of light. And every time a guest entered, the flames of the candles flickered and twisted themselves with the wind, struggling to keep erect. And Borghild's courage, too, rose and fell with the flickering motion of a flame which wrestles with the wind. Whenever the latch clicked she lifted her eyes and looked for Truls, and one moment she wished that she might never see his face again, and in the next she sent an eager glance toward the door. Presently he came, threw his fiddle on a bench, and with a reckless air walked up to her and held out his hand. She hesitated to return his greeting, but when she saw the deep lines of suffering in his face, her heart went forward with a great tenderness toward him, a tenderness such as one feels for a child who is sick, and suffers without hope of healing. She laid her hand in his, and there it lay for a while listlessly; for neither dared trust the joy which the sight of the other enkindled. But when she tried to draw her hand away, he caught it quickly, and with a sudden fervor of voice he said:

"The sight of you, Borghild, stills the hunger which is raging in my soul. Beware that you do not play with a life, Borghild, even though it be a worthless one."

There was something so hopelessly sad in his words, that they stung her to the quick. They laid bare a hidden deep in her heart, and she shrank back st the sight of her own vileness. How could she repair the injury she had done him? How could she heal the wound she had inflicted? A number of guests came up to greet her and among them Syvert Stein, a bold-looking young man, who, during that summer, had led her frequently in the dance. He had a square face, strong features, and a huge crop of towy hair. His race was far-famed for wit and daring.

"Tardy is your welcome, Borghild of Skogli," quoth he. "But what a faint heart does not give a bold hand can grasp, and what I am not offered I take unbidden."

So saying, he flung his arm about her waist, lifted her from the floor and put her down in the middle of the room. Truls stood and gazed at them with large, bewildered eyes. He tried hard to despise the braggart, but ended with envying him.

"Ha, fiddler, strike up a tune that shall ring through marrow and bone," shouted Syvert Stein, who struck the floor with his heels and moved his body to the measure of a spring-dance.

Truls still followed them with his eyes; suddenly he leaped up, and a wild thought burned in his breast. But with an effort he checked himself, grasped his violin, and struck a wailing chord of lament. Then he laid his ear close to the instrument, as if he were listening to some living voice hidden there within, ran warily with the bow over the strings, and warbled, and caroled, and sang with maddening glee, and still with a shivering undercurrent of woe. And the dusk which slept upon the black rafters was quickened and shook with the weird sound; every pulse in the wide hall beat more rapidly, and every eye kindled with a bolder fire. Presently{sic} a Strong male voice sang out to the measure of the violin:

"Come, fairest maid, tread the dance with me;
O heigh ho!"

And a clear, tremulous treble answered:

"So gladly tread I the dance with thee;
O heigh ho!"

Truls knew the voices only too well; it was Syvert Stein and Borghild who were singing a stave. [8]

Syvert--Like brier-roses thy red cheeks blush,
Borghild--And thine are rough like the thorny bush;

Both--An' a heigho!

Syvert--So fresh and green is the sunny lea;
O heigh ho!
Borghild--The fiddle twangeth so merrily;
O heigh ho!
Syvert--So lightly goeth the lusty reel,
Borghild--And round we whirl like a spinning-wheel;
Both--An' a heigho!

Syvert--Thine eyes are bright like the sunny fjord;
O heigh ho!
Borghild--And thine do flash like a Viking's sword;
O heigh ho!
Syvert--So lightly trippeth thy foot along,
Borghild--The air is teeming with joyful song;
Both--An' a heigh ho!

Syvert--Then fairest maid, while the woods are green,
O heigh ho!
Borghild--And thrushes sing the fresh leaves between;
O heigh ho!
Syvert--Come, let us dance in the gladsome day,
Borghild--Dance hate, and sorrow, and care away;
Both--An' a heigh ho!

The stave was at an end. The hot and flushed dancers straggled over the floor by twos and threes, and the big beer-horns were passed from hand to hand. Truls sat in his corner hugging his violin tightly to his bosom, only to do something, for he was vaguely afraid of himself--afraid of the thoughts that might rise--afraid of the deed they might prompt. He ran his fingers over his forehead, but he hardly felt the touch of his own hand. It was as if something was dead within him--as if a string had snapped in his breast, and left it benumbed and voiceless.

Presently he looked up and saw Borghild standing before him; she held her arms akimbo, her eyes shone with a strange light, and her features wore an air of recklessness mingled with pity.

"Ah, Borghild, is it you?" said he, in a hoarse voice. "What do you want with me? I thought you had done with me now."

"You are a very unwitty fellow," answered she, with a forced laugh. "The branch that does not bend must break."

She turned quickly on her heel and was lost in the crowd. He sat long pondering on her words, but their meaning remained hidden to him. The branch that does not bend must break. Was he the branch, and must he bend or break? By-and-by he put his hands on his knees, rose with a slow, uncertain motion, and stalked heavily toward the door. The fresh night air would do him good. The thought breathes more briskly in God's free nature, under the broad canopy of heaven. The white mist rose from the fields, and made the valley below appear like a white sea whose nearness you feel, even though you do not see it. And out of the mist the dark pines stretched their warning hands against the sky, and the moon was swimming, large and placid, between silvery islands of cloud. Truls began to beat his arms against his sides, and felt the warm blood spreading from his heart and thawing the numbness of his limbs. Not caring whither he went, he struck the path leading upward to the mountains. He took to humming an old air which happened to come into his head, only to try if there was life enough left in him to sing. It was the ballad of Young Kirsten and the Merman:

"The billows fall and the billows swell,
In the night so lone,
In the billows blue doth the merman dwell,
And strangely that harp was sounding."

He walked on briskly for a while, and, looking back upon the pain he had endured but a moment ago, he found it quite foolish and irrational. An absurd merriment took possession of him; but all the while he did not know where his foot stepped; his head swam, and his pulse beat feverishly. About midway between the forest and the mansion, where the field sloped more steeply, grew a clump of birch-trees, whose slender stems glimmered ghostly white in the moonlight. Something drove Truls to leave the beaten road, and, obeying the impulse, he steered toward the birches. A strange sound fell upon his ear, like the moan of one in distress. It did not startle him; indeed, he was in a mood when nothing could have caused him wonder. If the sky had suddenly tumbled down upon him, with moon and all, he would have taken it as a matter of course. Peering for a moment through the mist, he discerned the outline of a human figure. With three great strides he reached the birch-tree; at his feet sat Borghild rocking herself to and fro and weeping piteously. Without a word he seated himself at her side and tried to catch a glimpse of her face; but she hid it from him and went on sobbing. Still there could be no doubt that it was Borghild--one hour ago so merry, reckless, and defiant, now cowering at his feet and weeping like a broken-hearted child.

"Borghild," he said, at last, putting his arm gently about her waist, "you and I, I think, played together when we were children."

"So we did, Truls," answered she, struggling with her tears.

"And as we grew up, we spent many a pleasant hour with each other."

"Many a pleasant hour."

She raised her head, and he drew her more closely to him.

"But since then I have done you a great wrong," began she, after a while.

"Nothing done that cannot yet be undone," he took heart to answer.

It was long before her thoughts took shape, and, when at length they did, she dared not give them utterance. Nevertheless, she was all the time conscious of one strong desire, from which her conscience shrank as from a crime; and she wrestled ineffectually with her weakness until her weakness prevailed.

"I am glad you came," she faltered. "I knew you would come. There was something I wished to say to you."

"And what was it, Borghild?"

"I wanted to ask you to forgive me--"

"Forgive you--"

He sprang up as if something had stung him.

"And why not?" she pleaded, piteously.

"Ah, girl, you know not what you ask," cried he, with a sternness which startled her. "If I had more than one life to waste--but you caress with one hand and stab with the other. Fare thee well, Borghild, for here our paths separate."

He turned his back upon her and began to descend the slope.

"For God's sake, stay, Truls," implored she, and stretched her arms appealingly toward him; "tell me, oh, tell me all."

With a leap he was again at her side, stooped down over her, and, in a hoarse, passionate whisper, spoke the secret of his life in her ear. She gazed for a moment steadily into his face, then, in a few hurried words, she pledged him her love, her faith, her all. And in the stillness of that summer night they planned together their flight to a greater and freer land, where no world-old prejudice frowned upon the union of two kindred souls. They would wait in patience and silence until spring; then come the fresh winds from the ocean, and, with them, the birds of passage which awake the longings in the Norsemen's breasts, and the American vessels which give courage to many a sinking spirit, strength to the wearied arm, hope to the hopeless heart.

During that winter Truls and Borghild seldom saw each other. The parish was filled with rumors, and after the Christmas holiday it was told for certain that the proud maiden of Skogli had been promised in marriage to Syvert Stein. It was the general belief that the families had made the match, and that Borghild, at least, had hardly had any voice in the matter. Another report was that she had flatly refused to listen to any proposal from that quarter, and that, when she found that resistance was vain, she had cried three days and three nights, and refused to take any food. When this rumor reached the pastor's ear, he pronounced it an idle tale; "for," said he, "Borghild has always been a proper and well-behaved maiden, and she knows that she must honor father and mother, that it may be well with her, and she live long upon the land."

But Borghild sat alone in her gable window and looked longingly toward the ocean. The glaciers glittered, the rivers swelled, the buds of the forest burst, and great white sails began to glimmer on the far western horizon.

If Truls, the Nameless, as scoffers were wont to call him, had been a greater personage in the valley, it would, no doubt, have shocked the gossips to know that one fine morning he sold his cow, his gun and his dog, and wrapped sixty silver dollars in a leather bag, which he sewed fast to the girdle he wore about his waist. That same night some one was heard playing wildly up in the birch copse above the Skogli mansion; now it sounded like a wail of distress, then like a fierce, defiant laugh, and now again the music seemed to hush itself into a heart-broken, sorrowful moan, and the people crossed themselves, and whispered: "Our Father;" but Borghild sat at her gable window and listened long to the weird strain. The midnight came, but she stirred not. With the hour of midnight the music ceased. From the windows of hall and kitchen the light streamed out into the damp air, and the darkness stood like a wall on either side; within, maids and lads were busy brewing, baking, and washing, for in a week there was to be a wedding on the farm.

The week went and the wedding came. Truls had not closed his eyes all that night, and before daybreak he sauntered down along the beach and gazed out upon the calm fjord, where the white-winged sea-birds whirled in great airy surges around the bare crags. Far up above the noisy throng an ospray sailed on the blue expanse of the sky, and quick as thought swooped down upon a halibut which had ventured to take a peep at the rising sun. The huge fish struggled for a moment at the water's edge, then, with a powerful stroke of its tail, which sent the spray hissing through the air, dived below the surface. The bird of prey gave a loud scream, flapped fiercely with its broad wings, and for several minutes a thickening cloud of applauding ducks and seagulls and showers of spray hid the combat from the observer's eye. When the birds scattered, the ospray had vanished, and the waters again glittered calmly in the morning sun. Truls stood long, vacantly staring out upon the scene of the conflict, and many strange thoughts whirled through his head.

"Halloo, fiddler!" cried a couple of lads who had come to clear the wedding boats, "you are early on foot to-day. Here is a scoop. Come on and help us bail the boats."

Truls took the scoop, and looked at it as if he had never seen such a thing before; he moved about heavily, hardly knowing what he did, but conscious all the while of his own great misery. His limbs seemed half frozen, and a dull pain gathered about his head and in his breast--in fact, everywhere and nowhere.

About ten o'clock the bridal procession descended the slope to the fjord. Syvert Stein, the bridegroom, trod the earth with a firm, springy step, and spoke many a cheery word to the bride, who walked, silent and with downcast eyes, at his side. She wore the ancestral bridal crown on her head, and the little silver disks around its edge tinkled and shook as she walked. They hailed her with firing of guns and loud hurrahs as she stepped into the boat; still she did not raise her eyes, but remained silent. A small cannon, also an heir-loom in the family, was placed amidships, and Truls, with his violin, took his seat in the prow. A large solitary cloud, gold-rimmed but with thunder in its breast, sailed across the sky and threw its shadow over the bridal boat as it was pushed out from the shore, and the shadow fell upon the bride's countenance too; and when she lifted it, the mother of the bridegroom, who sat opposite her, shrank back, for the countenance looked hard, as if carved in stone--in the eyes a mute, hopeless appeal; on the lips a frozen prayer. The shadow of thunder upon a life that was opening--it was an ill omen, and its gloom sank into the hearts of the wedding guests. They spoke in undertones and threw pitying glances at the bride. Then at length Syvert Stein lost his patience.

"In sooth," cried he, springing up from his seat, "where is to-day the cheer that is wont to abide in the Norseman's breast? Methinks I see but sullen airs and ill-boding glances. Ha, fiddler, now move your strings lustily! None of your funeral airs, my lad, but a merry tune that shall sing through marrow and bone, and make the heart leap in the bosom."

Truls heard the words, and in a slow, mechanical way he took the violin out of its case and raised it to his chin. Syvert in the mean while put a huge silver beer-jug to his mouth, and, pledging his guests, emptied it even to the dregs. But the bride's cheek was pale; and it was so still in the boat that every man could hear his own breathing.

"Ha, to-day is Syvert Stein's wedding-day!" shouted the bridegroom, growing hot with wrath. "Let us try if the iron voice of the cannon can wake my guests from their slumber."

He struck a match and put it to the touch-hole of the cannon; a long boom rolled away over the surface of the waters and startled the echoes of the distant glaciers. A faint hurrah sounded from the nearest craft, but there came no response from the bridal boat. Syvert pulled the powder-horn from his pocket, laughed a wild laugh, and poured the whole contents of the horn into the mouth of the cannon.

"Now may the devil care for his own," roared he, and sprang up upon the row-bench. Then there came a low murmuring strain as of wavelets that ripple against a sandy shore. Borghild lifted her eyes, and they met those of the fiddler.

"Ah, I think I should rather be your bridegroom," whispered she, and a ray of life stole into her stony visage.

And she saw herself as a little rosy-cheeked girl sitting at his side on the beach fifteen years ago. But the music gathered strength from her glance, and onward it rushed through the noisy years of boyhood, shouting with wanton voice in the lonely glen, lowing with the cattle on the mountain pastures, and leaping like the trout at eventide in the brawling rapids; but through it all there ran a warm strain of boyish loyalty and strong devotion, and it thawed her frozen heart; for she knew that it was all for her and for her only. And it seemed such a beautiful thing, this long faithful life, which through sorrow and joy, through sunshine and gloom, for better for worse, had clung so fast to her. The wedding guests raised their heads, and a murmur of applause ran over the waters.

"Bravo!" cried the bridegroom. "Now at last the tongues are loosed."

Truls's gaze dwelt with tender sadness on the bride. Then came from the strings some airy quivering chords, faintly flushed like the petals of the rose, and fragrant like lilies of the valley; and they swelled with a strong, awakening life, and rose with a stormy fullness until they seemed on the point of bursting, when again they hushed themselves and sank into a low, disconsolate whisper. Once more the tones stretched out their arms imploringly, and again they wrestled despairingly with themselves, fled with a stern voice of warning, returned once more, wept, shuddered, and were silent.

"Beware that thou dost not play with a life!" sighed the bride, "even though it be a worthless one."

The wedding guests clapped their hands and shouted wildly against the sky. The bride's countenance burned with a strange feverish glow. The fiddler arose in the prow of the boat, his eyes flamed, he struck the strings madly, and the air trembled with melodious rapture. The voice of that music no living tongue can interpret. But the bride fathomed its meaning; her bosom labored vehemently, her lips quivered for an instant convulsively, and she burst into tears. A dark suspicion shot through the bridegroom's mind. He stared intently upon the weeping Borghild then turned his gaze to the fiddler, who, still regarding her, stood playing, with a half-frenzied look and motion.

"You cursed wretch!" shrieked Syvert, and made a leap over two benches to where Truls was standing. It came so unexpectedly that Truls had no time to prepare for defense; so he merely stretched out the hand in which he held the violin to ward off the blow which he saw was coming; but Syvert tore the instrument from his grasp and dashed it against the cannon, and, as it happened, just against the touch-hole. With a tremendous crash something black darted through the air and a white smoke brooded over the bridal boat. The bridegroom stood pale and stunned. At his feet lay Borghild--lay for a moment still, as if lifeless, then rose on her elbows, and a dark red current broke from her breast. The smoke scattered. No one saw how it was done; but a moment later Truls, the Nameless, lay kneeling at Borghild's side.

"It WAS a worthless life, beloved," whispered he, tenderly. "Now it is at an end."

And he lifted her up in his arms as one lifts a beloved child, pressed a kiss on her pale lips, and leaped into the water. Like lead they fell into the sea. A throng of white bubbles whirled up to the surface. A loud wail rose from the bridal fleet, and before the day was at an end it filled the valley; but the wail did not recall Truls, the Nameless, or Borghild his bride.

What life denied them, would to God that death may yield them!

ASATHOR'S VENGEANCE.

I.

IT was right up under the steel mountain wall where the farm of Kvaerk lay. How any man of common sense could have hit upon the idea of building a house there, where none but the goat and the hawk had easy access, had been, and I am afraid would ever be, a matter of wonder to the parish people. However, it was not Lage Kvaerk who had built the house, so he could hardly be made responsible for its situation. Moreover, to move from a place where one's life has once struck deep root, even if it be in the chinks and crevices of stones and rocks, is about the same as to destroy it. An old tree grows but poorly in a new soil. So Lage Kvaerk thought, and so he said, too, whenever his wife Elsie spoke of her sunny home at the river.

Gloomy as Lage usually was, he had his brighter moments, and people noticed that these were most likely to occur when Aasa, his daughter, was near. Lage was probably also the only being whom Aasa's presence could cheer; on other people it seemed to have the very opposite effect; for Aasa was--according to the testimony of those who knew her--the most peculiar creature that ever was born. But perhaps no one did know her; if her father was right, no one really did--at least no one but himself.

Aasa was all to her father; she was his past and she was his future, his hope and his life; and withal it must be admitted that those who judged her without knowing her had at least in one respect as just an opinion of her as he; for there was no denying that she was strange, very strange. She spoke when she ought to be silent, and was silent when it was proper to speak; wept when she ought to laugh, and laughed when it was proper to weep; but her laughter as well as her tears, her speech like her silence, seemed to have their source from within her own soul, to be occasioned, as it were, by something which no one else could see or hear. It made little difference where she was; if the tears came, she yielded to them as if they were something she had long desired in vain. Few could weep like her, and "weep like Aasa Kvaerk," was soon also added to the stock of parish proverbs. And then her laugh! Tears may be inopportune enough, when they come out of time, but laughter is far worse; and when poor Aasa once burst out into a ringing laughter in church, and that while the minister was pronouncing the benediction, it was only with the greatest difficulty that her father could prevent the indignant congregation from seizing her and carrying her before the sheriff for violation of the church-peace. Had she been poor and homely, then of course nothing could have saved her; but she happened to be both rich and beautiful, and to wealth and beauty much is pardoned. Aasa's beauty, however, was also of a very unusual kind; not the tame sweetness so common in her sex, but something of the beauty of the falcon, when it swoops down upon the un-watchful sparrow or soars round the lonely crags; something of the mystic depth of the dark tarn, when with bodeful trembling you gaze down into it, and see its weird traditions rise from its depth and hover over the pine-tops in the morning fog. Yet, Aasa was not dark; her hair was as fair and yellow as a wheat-field in August, her forehead high and clear, and her mouth and chin as if cut with a chisel; only her eyes were perhaps somewhat deeper than is common in the North, and the longer you looked at them the deeper they grew, just like the tarn, which, if you stare long enough into it, you will find is as deep as the heavens above, that is, whose depth only faith and fancy can fathom. But however long you looked at Aasa, you could never be quite sure that she looked at you; she seemed but to half notice whatever went on around her; the look of her eye was always more than half inward, and when it shone the brightest, it might well happen that she could not have told you how many years she had lived, or the name her father gave her in baptism.

Now Aasa was eighteen years old, and could knit, weave, and spin, and it was full time that wooers should come. "But that is the consequence of living in such an out-of-the-way place," said her mother; "who will risk his limbs to climb that neck-breaking rock? and the round-about way over the forest is rather too long for a wooer." Besides handling the loom and the spinning-wheel, Aasa had also learned to churn and make cheese to perfection, and whenever Elsie grieved at her strange behavior she always in the end consoled herself with the reflection that after all Aasa would make the man who should get her an excellent housewife.

The farm of Kvaerk was indeed most singularly situated. About a hundred feet from the house the rough wall of the mountain rose steep and threatening; and the most remarkable part of it was that the rock itself caved inward and formed a lofty arch overhead, which looked like a huge door leading into the mountain. Some short distance below, the slope of the fields ended in an abrupt precipice; far underneath lay the other farm-houses of the valley, scattered like small red or gray dots, and the river wound onward like a white silver stripe in the shelter of the dusky forest. There was a path down along the rock, which a goat or a brisk lad might be induced to climb, if the prize of the experiment were great enough to justify the hazard. The common road to Kvaerk made a large circuit around the forest, and reached the valley far up at its northern end.

It was difficult to get anything to grow at Kvaerk. In the spring all the valley lay bare and green, before the snow had begun to think of melting up there; and the night-frost would be sure to make a visit there, while the fields along the river lay silently drinking the summer dew. On such occasions the whole family at Kvaerk would have to stay up during all the night and walk back and forth on either side of the wheat-fields, carrying a long rope between them and dragging it slowly over the heads of the rye, to prevent the frost from settling; for as long as the ears could be kept in motion, they could not freeze. But what did thrive at Kvaerk in spite of both snow and night-frost was legends, and they throve perhaps the better for the very sterility of its material soil. Aasa of course had heard them all and knew them by heart; they had been her friends from childhood, and her only companions. All the servants, however, also knew them and many others besides, and if they were asked how the mansion of Kvaerk happened to be built like an eagle's nest on the brink of a precipice, they would tell you the following:

Saint Olaf, Norway's holy king, in the time of his youth had sailed as a Viking over the wide ocean, and in foreign lands had learned the doctrine of Christ the White. When he came home to claim the throne of his hereditary kingdom, he brought with him tapers and black priests, and commanded the people to over-throw the altars of Odin and Thor and to believe alone in Christ the White. If any still dared to slaughter a horse to the old gods, he cut off their ears, burned their farms, and drove them houseless from the smoking ruins. Here in the valley old Thor, or, as they called him, Asathor, had always helped us to vengeance and victory, and gentle Frey for many years had given us fair and fertile summers. Therefore the peasants paid little heed to King Olaf's god, and continued to bring their offerings to Odin and Asathor. This reached the king's ear, and he summoned his bishop and five black priests, and set out to visit our valley. Having arrived here, he called the peasants together, stood up on the Ting-stone, told them of the great things that the White Christ had done, and bade them choose between him and the old gods. Some were scared, and received baptism from the king's priests; others bit their lips and were silent; others again stood forth and told Saint Olaf that Odin and Asathor had always served them well, and that they were not going to give them up for Christ the White, whom they had never seen and of whom they knew nothing. The next night the red cock crew [9] over ten farms in the valley, and it happened to be theirs who had spoken against King Olaf's god. Then the peasants flocked to the Ting-stone and received the baptism of Christ the White. Some few, who had mighty kinsmen in the North, fled and spread the evil tidings. Only one neither fled nor was baptized, and that one was Lage Ulfson Kvaerk, the ancestor of the present Lage. He slew his best steed before Asathor's altar, and promised to give him whatever he should ask, even to his own life, if he would save him from the vengeance of the king. Asathor heard his prayer. As the sun set, a storm sprung up with thick darkness and gloom, the earth shook, Asathor drove his chariot over the heavens with deafening thunder and swung his hammer right and left, and the crackling lightning flew through the air like a hail-storm of fire. Then the peasants trembled, for they knew that Asathor was wroth. Only the king sat calm and fearless with his bishop and priests, quaffing the nut-brown mead. The tempest raged until morn. When the sun rose, Saint Olaf called his hundred swains, sprang into the saddle and rode down toward the river. Few men who saw the angry fire in his eye, and the frown on his royal brow, doubted whither he was bound. But having reached the ford, a wondrous sight met his eye. Where on the day before the highway had wound itself up the slope toward Lage Kvaerk's mansion, lay now a wild ravine; the rock was shattered into a thousand pieces, and a deep gorge, as if made by a single stroke of a huge hammer, separated the king from his enemy. Then Saint

Olaf made the sign of the cross, and mumbled the name of Christ the White; but his hundred swains made the sign of the hammer under their cloaks, and thought, Still is Asathor alive.

That same night Lage Ulfson Kvaerk slew a black ram, and thanked Asathor for his deliverance; and the Saga tells that while he was sprinkling the blood on the altar, the thundering god himself appeared to him, and wilder he looked than the fiercest wild Turk. Rams, said he, were every-day fare; they could redeem no promise. Brynhild, his daughter, was the reward Asathor demanded. Lage prayed and besought him to ask for something else. He would gladly give him one of his sons; for he had three sons, but only one daughter. Asathor was immovable; but so long Lage continued to beg, that at last he consented to come back in a year, when Lage perchance would be better reconciled to the thought of Brynhild's loss.

In the mean time King Olaf built a church to Christ the White on the headland at the river, where it stands until this day. Every evening, when the huge bell rumbled between the mountains, the parishioners thought they heard heavy, half-choked sighs over in the rocks at Kvaerk; and on Sunday mornings, when the clear-voiced chimes called them to high-mass, a suppressed moan would mingle with the sound of the bells, and die away with the last echo. Lage Ulfson was not the man to be afraid; yet the church-bells many a time drove the blood from his cheeks; for he also heard the moan from the mountain.

The year went, and Asathor returned. If he had not told his name, however, Lage would not have recognized him. That a year could work so great a change in a god, he would hardly have believed, if his own eyes had not testified to it. Asathor's cheeks were pale and bloodless, the lustre of his eye more than half quenched, and his gray hair hung in disorder down over his forehead.

"Methinks thou lookest rather poorly to-day," said Lage.

"It is only those cursed church-bells," answered the god; "they leave me no rest day or night."

"Aha," thought Lage, "if the king's bells are mightier than thou, then there is still hope of safety for my daughter."

"Where is Brynhild, thy daughter?" asked Asathor.

"I know not where she is," answered the father; and straightway he turned his eyes toward the golden cross that shone over the valley from Saint Olaf's steeple, and he called aloud on the White Christ's name. Then the god gave a fearful roar, fell on the ground, writhed and foamed and vanished into the mountain. In the next moment Lage heard a hoarse voice crying from within, "I shall return, Lage Ulfson, when thou shalt least expect me!"

Lage Ulfson then set to work clearing a way through the forest; and when that was done, he called all his household together, and told them of the power of Christ the White. Not long after he took his sons and his daughter, and hastened with them southward, until he found King Olaf. And, so the Saga relates, they all fell down on their knees before him, prayed for his forgiveness, and received baptism from the king's own bishop.

So ends the Saga of Lage Ulfson Kvaerk.

II.

Aasa Kvaerk loved her father well, but especially in the winter. Then, while she sat turning her spinning-wheel in the light of the crackling logs, his silent presence always had a wonderfully soothing and calming effect upon her. She never laughed then, and seldom wept; when she felt his eyes resting on her, her thoughts, her senses, and her whole being seemed by degrees to be lured from their hiding-place and concentrate on him; and from him they ventured again, first timidly, then more boldly, to grasp the objects around him. At such times Aasa could talk and jest almost like other girls, and her mother, to whom "other girls" represented the ideal of womanly perfection, would send significant glances, full of hope and encouragement, over to Lage, and he would quietly nod in return, as if to say that he entirely agreed with her. Then Elsie had bright visions of wooers and thrifty housewives, and even Lage dreamed of seeing the ancient honor of the family re-established. All depended on Aasa. She was the last of the mighty race. But when summer came, the bright visions fled; and the spring winds, which to others bring life and joy, to Kvaerk brought nothing but sorrow. No sooner had the mountain brooks begun to swell, than Aasa began to laugh and to weep; and when the first birches budded up in the glens, she could no longer be kept at home. Prayers and threats were equally useless. From early dawn until evening she would roam about in forests and fields, and when late at night she stole into the room and slipped away into some corner, Lage drew a deep sigh and thought of the old tradition.

Aasa was nineteen years old before she had a single wooer. But when she was least expecting it, the wooer came to her.

It was late one summer night; the young maiden was sitting on the brink of the ravine, pondering on the old legend and peering down into the deep below. It was not the first time she had found her way hither, where but seldom a human foot had dared to tread. To her every alder and bramble-bush, that clothed the naked wall of the rock, were as familiar as were the knots and veins in the ceiling of the chamber where from her childhood she had slept; and as she sat there on the brink of the precipice, the late summer sun threw its red lustre upon her and upon the fogs that came drifting up from the deep. With her eyes she followed the drifting masses of fog, and wondered, as they rose higher and higher, when they would reach her; in her fancy she saw herself dancing over the wide expanse of heaven, clad in the sun-gilded evening fogs; and Saint Olaf, the great and holy king, came riding to meet her, mounted on a flaming steed made of the glory of a thousand sunsets; then Saint Olaf took her hand and lifted her up, and she sat with him on the flaming steed: but the fog lingered in the deep below, and as it rose it spread like a thin, half-invisible gauze over the forests and the fields, and at last vanished into the infinite space. But hark! a huge stone rolls down over the mountain-side, then another, and another; the noise grows, the birches down there in the gorge tremble and shake. Aasa leaned out over the brink of the ravine, and, as far as she could distinguish anything from her dizzying height, thought she saw something gray creeping slowly up the neck-breaking mountain path; she watched it for a while, but as it seemed to advance no farther she again took refuge in her reveries. An hour might have passed, or perhaps more, when suddenly she heard a noise only a few feet distant, and, again stooping out over the brink, saw the figure of a man struggling desperately to climb the last great ledge of the rock. With both his hands he clung to a little birch-tree which stretched its slender arms down over the black wall, but with every moment that passed seemed less likely to accomplish the feat. The girl for a while stood watching him with unfeigned curiosity, then, suddenly reminding herself that the situation to him must be a dangerous one, seized hold of a tree that grew near the brink, and leaned out over the rock to give him her assistance. He eagerly grasped her extended hand, and with a vigorous pull she flung him up on the grassy level, where he remained lying for a minute or two, apparently utterly unable to account for his sudden ascent, and gazing around him with a half-frightened, half-bewildered look. Aasa, to whom his appearance was no less strange than his demeanor, unluckily hit upon the idea that perhaps her rather violent treatment had momentarily stunned him, and when, as answer to her sympathizing question if he was hurt, the stranger abruptly rose to his feet and towered up before her to the formidable height of six feet four or five, she could no longer master her mirth, but burst out into a most vehement fit of laughter. He stood calm and silent, and looked at her with a timid but strangely bitter smile. He was so very different from any man she had ever seen before; therefore she laughed, not necessarily because he amused her, but because his whole person was a surprise to her; and there he stood, tall and gaunt and timid, and said not a word, only gazed and gazed. His dress was not the national costume of the valley, neither was it like anything that Aasa had ever known. On his head he wore a cap that hung all on one side, and was decorated with a long, heavy silk tassel. A threadbare coat, which seemed to be made expressly not to fit him, hung loosely on his sloping shoulders, and a pair of gray pantaloons, which were narrow where they ought to have been wide, and wide where it was their duty to be narrow, extended their service to a little more than the upper half of the limb, and, by a kind of compromise with the tops of the boots, managed to protect also the lower half. His features were delicate, and would have been called handsome had they belonged to a proportionately delicate body; in his eyes hovered a dreamy vagueness which seemed to come and vanish, and to flit from one feature to another, suggesting the idea of remoteness, and a feeling of hopeless strangeness to the world and all its concerns.

"Do I inconvenience you, madam?" were the first words he uttered, as Aasa in her usual abrupt manner stayed her laughter, turned her back on him, and hastily started for the house.

"Inconvenience?" said she, surprised, and again slowly turned on her heel; "no, not that I know."

"Then tell me if there are people living here in the neighborhood, or if the light deceived me, which I saw from the other side of the river."

"Follow me," answered Aasa, and she naively reached him her hand; "my father's name is Lage Ulfson Kvaerk; he lives in the large house you see straight before you, there on the hill; and my mother lives there too."

And hand in hand they walked together, where a path had been made between two adjoining rye-fields; his serious smile seemed to grow milder and happier, the longer he lingered at her side, and her eye caught a ray of more human intelligence, as it rested on him.

"What do you do up here in the long winter?" asked he, after a pause.

"We sing," answered she, as it were at random, because the word came into her mind; "and what do you do, where you come from?"

"I gather song."

"Have you ever heard the forest sing?" asked she, curiously.

"That is why I came here."

And again they walked on in silence.

It was near midnight when they entered the large hall at Kvaerk. Aasa went before, still leading the young man by the hand. In the twilight which filled the house, the space between the black, smoky rafters opened a vague vista into the region of the fabulous, and every object in the room loomed forth from the dusk with exaggerated form and dimensions. The room appeared at first to be but the haunt of the spirits of the past; no human voice, no human footstep, was heard; and the stranger instinctively pressed the hand he held more tightly; for he was not sure but that he was standing on the boundary of dream-land, and some elfin maiden had reached him her hand to lure him into her mountain, where he should live with her forever. But the illusion was of brief duration; for Aasa's thoughts had taken a widely different course; it was but seldom she had found herself under the necessity of making a decision; and now it evidently devolved upon her to find the stranger a place of rest for the night; so instead of an elf-maid's kiss and a silver palace, he soon found himself huddled into a dark little alcove in the wall, where he was told to go to sleep, while Aasa wandered over to the empty cow-stables, and threw herself down in the hay by the side of two sleeping milkmaids.

III.

There was not a little astonishment manifested among the servant-maids at Kvaerk the next morning, when the huge, gaunt figure of a man was seen to launch forth from Aasa's alcove, and the strangest of all was, that Aasa herself appeared to be as much astonished as the rest. And there they stood, all gazing at the bewildered traveler, who indeed was no less startled than they, and as utterly unable to account for his own sudden apparition. After a long pause, he summoned all his courage, fixed his eyes intently on the group of the girls, and with a few rapid steps advanced toward Aasa, whom he seized by the hand and asked, "Are you not my maiden of yester-eve?"

She met his gaze firmly, and laid her hand on her forehead as if to clear her thoughts; as the memory of the night flashed through her mind, a bright smile lit up her features, and she answered, "You are the man who gathers song. Forgive me, I was not sure but it was all a dream; for I dream so much."

Then one of the maids ran out to call Lage Ulfson, who had gone to the stables to harness the horses; and he came and greeted the unknown man, and thanked him for last meeting, as is the wont of Norse peasants, although they had never seen each other until that morning. But when the stranger had eaten two meals in Lage's house, Lage asked him his name and his father's occupation; for old Norwegian hospitality forbids the host to learn the guest's name before he has slept and eaten under his roof. It was that same afternoon, when they sat together smoking their pipes under the huge old pine in the yard,--it was then Lage inquired about the young man's name and family; and the young man said that his name was Trond Vigfusson, that he had graduated at the University of Christiania, and that his father had been a lieutenant in the army; but both he and Trond's mother had died, when Trond was only a few years old. Lage then told his guest Vigfusson something about his family, but of the legend of Asathor and Saint Olaf he spoke not a word. And while they were sitting there talking together, Aasa came and sat down at Vigfusson's feet; her long golden hair flowed in a waving stream down over her back and shoulders, there was a fresh, healthful glow on her cheeks, and her blue, fathomless eyes had a strangely joyous, almost triumphant expression. The father's gaze dwelt fondly upon her, and the collegian was but conscious of one thought: that she was wondrously beautiful. And still so great was his natural timidity and awkwardness in the presence of women, that it was only with the greatest difficulty he could master his first impulse to find some excuse for leaving her. She, however, was aware of no such restraint.

"You said you came to gather song," she said; "where do you find it? for I too should like to find some new melody for my old thoughts; I have searched so long."

"I find my songs on the lips of the people," answered he, "and I write them down as the maidens or the old men sing them."

She did not seem quite to comprehend that. "Do you hear maidens sing them?" asked she, astonished. "Do you mean the troll-virgins and the elf-maidens?"

"By troll-virgins and elf-maidens, or what the legends call so, I understand the hidden and still audible voices of nature, of the dark pine forests, the legend-haunted glades, and the silent tarns; and this was what I referred to when I answered your question if I had ever heard the forest sing."

"Oh, oh!" cried she, delighted, and clapped her hands like a child; but in another moment she as suddenly grew serious again, and sat steadfastly gazing into his eye, as if she were trying to look into his very soul and there to find something kindred to her own lonely heart. A minute ago her presence had embarrassed him; now, strange to say, he met her eye, and smiled happily as he met it.

"Do you mean to say that you make your living by writing songs?" asked Lage.

"The trouble is," answered Vigfusson, "that I make no living at all; but I have invested a large capital, which is to yield its interest in the future. There is a treasure of song hidden in every nook and corner of our mountains and forests, and in our nation's heart. I am one of the miners who have come to dig it out before time and oblivion shall have buried every trace of it, and there shall not be even the will-o'-the-wisp of a legend to hover over the spot, and keep alive the sad fact of our loss and our blamable negligence."

Here the young man paused; his eyes gleamed, his pale cheeks flushed, and there was a warmth and an enthusiasm in his words which alarmed Lage, while on Aasa it worked like the most potent charm of the ancient mystic runes; she hardly comprehended more than half of the speaker's meaning, but his fire and eloquence were on this account none the less powerful.

"If that is your object," remarked Lage, "I think you have hit upon the right place in coming here. You will be able to pick up many an odd bit of a story from the servants and others hereabouts, and you are welcome to stay here with us as long as you choose."

Lage could not but attribute to Vigfusson the merit of having kept Aasa at home a whole day, and that in the month of midsummer. And while he sat there listening to their conversation, while he contemplated the delight that beamed from his daughter's countenance and, as he thought, the really intelligent expression of her eyes, could he conceal from himself the paternal hopes that swelled his heart? She was all that was left him, the life or the death of his mighty race. And here was one who was likely to understand her, and to whom she seemed willing to yield all the affection of her warm but wayward heart. Thus ran Lage Ulfson's reflections; and at night he had a little consultation with Elsie, his wife, who, it is needless to add, was no less sanguine than he.

"And then Aasa will make an excellent housewife, you know," observed Elsie. "I will speak to the girl about it to-morrow."

"No, for Heaven's sake, Elsie!" exclaimed Lage, "don't you know your daughter better than that? Promise me, Elsie, that you will not say a single word; it would be a cruel thing, Elsie, to mention anything to her. She is not like other girls, you know."

"Very well, Lage, I shall not say a single word. Alas, you are right, she is not like other girls." And Elsie again sighed at her husband's sad ignorance of a woman's nature, and at the still sadder fact of her daughter's inferiority to the accepted standard of womanhood.

IV.

Trond Vigfusson must have made a rich harvest of legends at Kvaerk, at least judging by the time he stayed there; for days and weeks passed, and he had yet said nothing of going. Not that anybody wished him to go; no, on the contrary, the longer he stayed the more indispensable he seemed to all; and Lage Ulfson could hardly think without a shudder of the possibility of his ever having to leave them. For Aasa, his only child, was like another being in the presence of this stranger; all that weird, forest-like intensity, that wild, half supernatural tinge in her character which in a measure excluded her from the blissful feeling of fellowship with other men, and made her the strange, lonely creature she was,--all this seemed to vanish as dew in the morning sun when Vigfusson's eyes rested upon her; and with every day that passed, her human and womanly nature gained a stronger hold upon her. She followed him like his shadow on all his wanderings, and when they sat down together by the wayside, she would sing, in a clear, soft voice, an ancient lay or ballad, and he would catch her words on his paper, and smile at the happy prospect of perpetuating what otherwise would have been lost. Aasa's love, whether conscious or not, was to him an everlasting source of strength, was a revelation of himself to himself, and a clearing and widening power which brought ever more and more of the universe within the scope of his vision. So they lived on from day to day and from week to week, and, as old Lage remarked, never had Kvaerk been the scene of so much happiness. Not a single time during Vigfusson's stay had Aasa fled to the forest, not a meal had she missed, and at the hours for family devotion she had taken her seat at the big table with the rest and apparently listened with as much attention and interest. Indeed, all this time Aasa seemed purposely to avoid the dark haunts of the woods, and, whenever she could, chose the open highway; not even Vigfusson's entreaties could induce her to tread the tempting paths that led into the forest's gloom.

"And why not, Aasa?" he would say; "summer is ten times summer there when the drowsy noonday spreads its trembling maze of shadows between those huge, venerable trunks. You can feel the summer creeping into your very heart and soul, there!"

"Oh, Vigfusson," she would answer, shaking her head mournfully, "for a hundred paths that lead in, there is only one that leads out again, and sometimes even that one is nowhere to be found."

He understood her not, but fearing to ask, he remained silent.

His words and his eyes always drew her nearer and nearer to him; and the forest and its strange voices seemed a dark, opposing influence, which strove to take possession of her heart and to wrest her away from him forever; she helplessly clung to him; every thought and emotion of her soul clustered about him, and every hope of life and happiness was staked on him.

One evening Vigfusson and old Lage Ulfson had been walking about the fields to look at the crop, both smoking their evening pipes. But as they came down toward the brink whence the path leads between the two adjoining rye-fields, they heard a sweet, sad voice crooning some old ditty down between the birch-trees at the precipice; they stopped to listen, and soon recognized Aasa's yellow hair over the tops the rye; the shadow as of a painful emotion flitted over the father's countenance, and he turned his back on his guest and started to go; then again paused, and said, imploringly, "Try to get her home if you can, friend Vigfusson."

Vigfusson nodded, and Lage went; the song had ceased for a moment, now it began again:

> "Ye twittering birdlings, in forest and glen
> I have heard you so gladly before;
> But a bold knight hath come to woo me,
> I dare listen to you no more.
> For it is so dark, so dark in the forest.
>
> "And the knight who hath come a-wooing to me,
> He calls me his love and his own;
> Why then should I stray through the darksome woods,
> Or dream in the glades alone?
> For it is so dark, so dark in the forest."

Her voice fell to a low unintelligible murmur; then it rose, and the last verses came, clear, soft, and low, drifting on the evening breeze:

> "Yon beckoning world, that shimmering lay
> O'er the woods where the old pines grow,
> That gleamed through the moods of the summer day
> When the breezes were murmuring low
> (And it is so dark, so dark in the forest);

"Oh let me no more in the sunshine hear
Its quivering noonday call;
The bold knight's love is the sun of my heart--
Is my life, and my all in all.
But it is so dark, so dark in the forest."

The young man felt the blood rushing to his face--his heart beat violently. There was a keen sense of guilt in the blush on his cheek, a loud accusation in the throbbing pulse and the swelling heart-beat. Had he not stood there behind the maiden's back and cunningly peered into her soul's holy of holies? True, he loved Aasa; at least he thought he did, and the conviction was growing stronger with every day that passed. And now he had no doubt that he had gained her heart. It was not so much the words of the ballad which had betrayed the secret; he hardly knew what it was, but somehow the truth had flashed upon him, and he could no longer doubt.

Vigfusson sat down on the moss-grown rock and pondered. How long he sat there he did not know, but when he rose and looked around, Aasa was gone. Then remembering her father's request to bring her home, he hastened up the hill-side toward the mansion, and searched for her in all directions. It was near midnight when he returned to Kvaerk, where Aasa sat in her high gable window, still humming the weird melody of the old ballad.

By what reasoning Vigfusson arrived at his final conclusion is difficult to tell. If he had acted according to his first and perhaps most generous impulse, the matter would soon have been decided; but he was all the time possessed of a vague fear of acting dishonorably, and it was probably this very fear which made him do what, to the minds of those whose friendship and hospitality he had accepted, had something of the appearance he wished so carefully to avoid. Aasa was rich; he had nothing; it was a reason for delay, but hardly a conclusive one. They did not know him; he must go out in the world and prove himself worthy of her. He would come back when he should have compelled the world to respect him; for as yet he had done nothing. In fact, his arguments were good and honorable enough, and there would have been no fault to find with him, had the object of his love been as capable of reasoning as he was himself. But Aasa, poor thing, could do nothing by halves; a nature like hers brooks no delay; to her love was life or it was death.

The next morning he appeared at breakfast with his knapsack on his back, and otherwise equipped for his journey. It was of no use that Elsie cried and begged him to stay, that Lage joined his prayers to hers, and that Aasa stood staring at him with a bewildered gaze. Vigfusson shook hands with them all, thanked them for their kindness to him, and promised to return; he held Aasa's hand long in his, but when he released it, it dropped helplessly at her side.

V.

Far up in the glen, about a mile from Kvaerk, ran a little brook; that is, it was little in summer and winter, but in the spring, while the snow was melting up in the mountains, it overflowed the nearest land and turned the whole glen into a broad and shallow river. It was easy to cross, however; a light foot might jump from stone to stone, and be over in a minute. Not the hind herself could be lighter on her foot than Aasa was; and even in the spring-flood it was her wont to cross and recross the brook, and to sit dreaming on a large stone against which the water broke incessantly, rushing in white torrents over its edges.

Here she sat one fair summer day--the day after Vigfusson's departure. It was noon, and the sun stood high over the forest. The water murmured and murmured, babbled and whispered, until at length there came a sudden unceasing tone into its murmur, then another, and it sounded like a faint whispering song of small airy beings. And as she tried to listen, to fix the air in her mind, it all ceased again, and she heard but the monotonous murmuring of the brook. Everything seemed so empty and worthless, as if that faint melody had been the world of the moment. But there it was again; it sung and sung, and the birch overhead took up the melody and rustled it with its leaves, and the grasshopper over in the grass caught it and whirred it with her wings. The water, the trees, the air, were full of it. What a strange melody!

Aasa well knew that every brook and river has its Neck, besides hosts of little water-sprites. She had heard also that in the moonlight at midsummer, one might chance to see them rocking in bright little shells, playing among the pebbles, or dancing on the large leaves of the water-lily. And that they could sing also, she doubted not; it was their voices she heard through the murmuring of the brook. Aasa eagerly bent forward and gazed down into the water: the faint song grew louder, paused suddenly, and sprang into life again; and its sound was so sweet, so wonderfully alluring! Down there in the water, where a stubborn pebble kept chafing a precipitous little side current, clear tiny pearl-drops would leap up from the stream, and float half-wonderingly downward from rapid to rapid, until they lost themselves in the whirl of some stronger current. Thus sat Aasa and gazed and gazed, and in one moment she seemed to see what in the next moment she saw not. Then a sudden great hush stole through the forest, and in the hush she could hear the silence calling her name. It was so long since she had been in the forest, it seemed ages and ages ago. She hardly knew herself; the light seemed to be shining into her eyes as with a will and purpose, perhaps to obliterate something, some old dream or memory, or to impart some new power--the power of seeing the unseen. And this very thought, this fear of some possible loss, brought the fading memory back, and she pressed her hands against her throbbing temples as if to bind and chain it there forever; and it was he to whom her thought returned. She heard his voice, saw him beckoning to her to follow him, and she rose to obey, but her limbs were as petrified, and the stone on which she was sitting held her with the power of a hundred strong arms. The sunshine smote upon her eyelids, and his name was blotted out from her life; there was nothing but emptiness all around her. Gradually the forest drew nearer and nearer, the water bubbled and rippled, and the huge, bare-stemmed pines stretched their long gnarled arms toward her. The birches waved their heads with a wistful nod, and the profile of the rock grew into a face with a long, hooked nose, and a mouth half open as if to speak. And the word that trembled on his lips was, "Come." She felt no fear nor reluctance, but rose to obey. Then and not until then she saw an old man standing at her side; his face was the face of the rock, his white beard flowed to his girdle, and his mouth was half open, but no word came from his lips. There was something in the wistful look of his eye which she knew so well, which she had seen so often, although she could not tell when or where. The old man extended his hand; Aasa took it, and fearlessly or rather spontaneously followed. They approached the steep, rocky wall; as they drew near, a wild, fierce laugh rang through the forest. The features of the old man were twisted as it were into a grin; so also were the features of the rock; but the laugh blew like a mighty blast through the forest.

Aasa clung to the old man's hand and followed him--she knew not whither.

At home in the large sitting-room at Kvaerk sat Lage, brooding over the wreck of his hopes and his happiness. Aasa had gone to the woods again the very first day after Vigfusson's departure. What would be the end of all this? It was already late in the evening, and she had not returned. The father cast anxious glances toward the door, every time he heard the latch moving. At last, when it was near midnight, he roused all his men from their sleep, and commanded them to follow him. Soon the dusky forests resounded far and near with the blast of horns, the report of guns, and the calling and shouting of men. The affrighted stag crossed and recrossed the path of the hunters, but not a rifle was leveled at its head. Toward morning--it was before the sun had yet risen--Lage, weary and stunned, stood leaning up against a huge fir. Then suddenly a fierce, wild laugh rang through the forest. Lage shuddered, raised his hand slowly and pressed it hard against his forehead, vainly struggling to clear his thoughts. The men clung fearfully together; a few of the more courageous ones drew their knives and made the sign of the cross with them in the air. Again the same mad laugh shook the air, and swept over the crowns of the pine-trees. Then Lage lifted his eyes toward heaven and wrung his hands: for the awful truth stood before him. He remained a long while leaning against that old fir as in a dead stupor; and no one dared to arouse him. A suppressed murmur reached the men's ears. "But deliver us from evil" were the last words they heard.

When Lage and his servants came home to Kvaerk with the mournful tidings of Aasa's disappearance, no one knew what to do or say. There could be no doubt that Aasa was "mountain-taken," as they call it; for there were Trolds and dwarfs in all the rocks and forests round about, and they would hardly let slip the chance of alluring so fair a maiden as Aasa was into their castles in the mountains. Elsie, her mother, knew a good deal about the Trolds, their tricks, and their way of living, and when she had wept her fill, she fell to thinking of the possibility of regaining her daughter from their power. If Aasa had not yet tasted of food or drink in the mountain, she was still out of danger; and if the pastor would allow the church-bell to be brought up into the forest and rung near the rock where the laugh had been heard, the Trolds could be compelled to give her back. No sooner had this been suggested to Lage, than the command was given to muster the whole force of men and horses, and before evening on the same day the sturdy swains of Kvaerk were seen climbing the tower of the venerable church, whence soon the huge old bell descended, to the astonishment of the throng of curious women and children who had flocked together to see the extraordinary sight. It was laid upon four large wagons, which had been joined together with ropes and planks, and drawn away by twelve strong horses. Long after the strange caravan had vanished in the twilight, the children stood gazing up into the empty bell-tower.

It was near midnight, when Lage stood at the steep, rocky wall in the forest; the men were laboring to hoist the church-bell up to a staunch cross-beam between two mighty fir-trees, and in the weird light of their torches, the wild surroundings looked wilder and more fantastic. Anon, the muffled noise and bustle of the work being at an end, the laborers withdrew, and a strange, feverish silence seemed to brood over the forest. Lage took a step forward, and seized the bell-rope; the clear, conquering toll of the metal rung solemnly through the silence, and from the rocks, the earth, and the tree-tops, rose a fierce chorus of howls, groans, and screams. All night the ringing continued; the old trees swayed to and fro, creaked, and groaned, the roots loosened their holds in the fissures of the rock, and the bushy crowns bowed low under their unwonted burden.

It was well-nigh morn, but the dense fog still brooded over the woods, and it was dark as night. Lage was sitting on the ground, his head leaning on both his elbows; at his side lay the flickering torch, and the huge bell hung dumb overhead. In the dark he felt a hand touch his shoulder; had it happened only a few hours before, he would have shuddered; now the physical sensation hardly communicated itself to his mind, or, if it did, had no power to rouse him from his dead, hopeless apathy. Suddenly--could he trust his own ears?--the church-bell gave a slow, solemn, quivering stroke, and the fogs rolled in thick masses to the east and to the west, as if blown by the breath of the sound. Lage seized his torch, sprang to his feet, and saw--Vigfusson. He stretched his arm with the blazing torch closer to the young man's face, stared at him with large eyes, and his lip quivered; but he could not utter a word.

"Vigfusson?" faltered he at last.

"It is I;" and the second stroke followed, stronger and more solemn than the first. The same fierce, angry voices chorused forth from every nook of the rock and the woods. Then came the third--the noise grew; fourth--and it sounded like a hoarse, angry hiss; when the twelfth stroke fell, silence reigned again in the forest. Vigfusson dropped the bell-rope, and with a loud voice called Lage Kvaerk and his men. He lit a torch, held it aloft over his head, and peered through the dusky night. The men spread through the highlands to search for the lost maiden; Lage followed close in Vigfusson's footsteps. They had not walked far when they heard the babbling of the brook only a few feet away. Thither they directed their steps. On a large stone in the middle of the stream the youth thought he saw something white, like a large kerchief. Quick as thought he was at its side, bowed down with his torch, and--fell backward. It was Aasa, his beloved, cold and dead; but as the father stooped over his dead child the same mad laugh echoed wildly throughout the wide woods, but madder and louder than ever before, and from the rocky wall came a fierce, broken voice:

"I came at last."

When, after an hour of vain search, the men returned to the place whence they had started, they saw a faint light flickering between the birches not fifty feet away; they formed a firm column, and with fearful hearts drew nearer. There lay Lage Kvaerk, their master, still bending down over his child's pale features, and staring into her sunken eyes as if he could not believe that she were really dead. And at his side stood Vigfusson, pale and aghast, with the burning torch in his hand. The footsteps of the men awakened the father, but when he turned his face on them they shuddered and started back. Then Lage rose, lifted the maiden from the stone, and silently laid her in Vigfusson's arms; her rich yellow hair flowed down over his shoulder. The youth let his torch fall into the waters, and with a sharp, serpent-like hiss its flame was quenched. He crossed the brook; the men followed, and the dark pine-trees closed over the last descendant of Lage Ulfson's mighty race.

Notes:

[1] "I am a Dane. I speak Danish."

[2] Examen artium is the entrance examination to the Norwegian University, and philosophicum the first degree. The ranks given at these are Laudabilis prae ceteris (in student's parlance, prae), laudabilis or laud, haud illaudabilis, or haud, etc.

[3] Free translation of a Swedish serenade, the name of whose author I have forgotten. H. H. B.

[4] Translation, from "Exotics. By J. F. C. & C. L."

[5] In the country districts of Norway Saturday evening is regarded as "the wooer's eve."

[6] The saeter is a place in the mountains where the Norwegian peasants spend their summers pasturing their cattle. Every large farm has its own saeter, consisting of one or more chalets, hedged in by a fence of stone or planks.

[7] Katzenjammer is the sensation a man has the morning after a carousal.

[8] A stave is an improvised responsive song. It is an ancient pastime in Norway, and is kept up until this day, especially among the peasantry. The students, also, at their social gatherings, throw improvised rhymes to each other across the table, and the rest of the company repeat the refrain.

[9] "The red cock crew" is the expression used in the old Norwegian Fagas for incendiary fire.

The Codes Of Hammurabi And Moses
W. W. Davies

QTY

The discovery of the Hammurabi Code is one of the greatest achievements of archaeology, and is of paramount interest, not only to the student of the Bible, but also to all those interested in ancient history...

Religion   **ISBN:** *1-59462-338-4*   **Pages:132**

MSRP $12.95

The Theory of Moral Sentiments
Adam Smith

QTY

This work from 1749. contains original theories of conscience amd moral judgment and it is the foundation for systemof morals.

Philosophy **ISBN:** *1-59462-777-0*   **Pages:536**

MSRP $19.95

Jessica's First Prayer
Hesba Stretton

QTY

In a screened and secluded corner of one of the many railway-bridges which span the streets of London there could be seen a few years ago, from five o'clock every morning until half past eight, a tidily set-out coffee-stall, consisting of a trestle and board, upon which stood two large tin cans, with a small fire of charcoal burning under each so as to keep the coffee boiling during the early hours of the morning when the work-people were thronging into the city on their way to their daily toil...

Pages:84

Childrens   **ISBN:** *1-59462-373-2*   *MSRP $9.95*

My Life and Work
Henry Ford

QTY

Henry Ford revolutionized the world with his implementation of mass production for the Model T automobile. Gain valuable business insight into his life and work with his own auto-biography... "We have only started on our development of our country we have not as yet, with all our talk of wonderful progress, done more than scratch the surface. The progress has been wonderful enough but..."

Pages:300

Biographies/   **ISBN:** *1-59462-198-5*   *MSRP $21.95*

The Art of Cross-Examination
Francis Wellman

I presume it is the experience of every author, after his first book is published upon an important subject, to be almost overwhelmed with a wealth of ideas and illustrations which could readily have been included in his book, and which to his own mind, at least, seem to make a second edition inevitable. Such certainly was the case with me; and when the first edition had reached its sixth impression in five months, I rejoiced to learn that it seemed to my publishers that the book had met with a sufficiently favorable reception to justify a second and considerably enlarged edition. ..

Pages:412

Reference   ISBN: *1-59462-647-2*   *MSRP $19.95*

On the Duty of Civil Disobedience
Henry David Thoreau

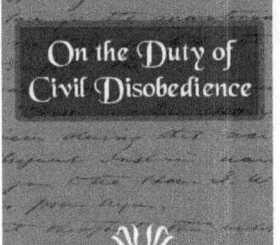

Thoreau wrote his famous essay, On the Duty of Civil Disobedience, as a protest against an unjust but popular war and the immoral but popular institution of slave-owning. He did more than write—he declined to pay his taxes, and was hauled off to gaol in consequence. Who can say how much this refusal of his hastened the end of the war and of slavery ?

Law   ISBN: *1-59462-747-9*   **Pages:48**

MSRP $7.45

Dream Psychology Psychoanalysis for Beginners
Sigmund Freud

Sigmund Freud, born Sigismund Schlomo Freud (May 6, 1856 - September 23, 1939), was a Jewish-Austrian neurologist and psychiatrist who co-founded the psychoanalytic school of psychology. Freud is best known for his theories of the unconscious mind, especially involving the mechanism of repression; his redefinition of sexual desire as mobile and directed towards a wide variety of objects; and his therapeutic techniques, especially his understanding of transference in the therapeutic relationship and the presumed value of dreams as sources of insight into unconscious desires.

Pages:196

Psychology   ISBN: *1-59462-905-6*   *MSRP $15.45*

The Miracle of Right Thought
Orison Swett Marden

Believe with all of your heart that you will do what you were made to do. When the mind has once formed the habit of holding cheerful, happy, prosperous pictures, it will not be easy to form the opposite habit. It does not matter how improbable or how far away this realization may see, or how dark the prospects may be, if we visualize them as best we can, as vividly as possible, hold tenaciously to them and vigorously struggle to attain them, they will gradually become actualized, realized in the life. But a desire, a longing without endeavor, a yearning abandoned or held indifferently will vanish without realization.

Pages:360

Self Help   ISBN: *1-59462-644-8*   *MSRP $25.45*

☐ **The Rosicrucian Cosmo-Conception Mystic Christianity** *by Max Heindel*　ISBN: *1-59462-188-8*　**$38.95**
The Rosicrucian Cosmo-conception is not dogmatic, neither does it appeal to any other authority than the reason of the student. It is: not controversial, but is: sent forth in the, hope that it may help to clear...　New Age/Religion Pages 646

☐ **Abandonment To Divine Providence** *by Jean-Pierre de Caussade*　ISBN: *1-59462-228-0*　**$25.95**
"The Rev. Jean Pierre de Caussade was one of the most remarkable spiritual writers of the Society of Jesus in France in the 18th Century. His death took place at Toulouse in 1751. His works have gone through many editions and have been republished...　Inspirational/Religion Pages 400

☐ **Mental Chemistry** *by Charles Haanel*　ISBN: *1-59462-192-6*　**$23.95**
Mental Chemistry allows the change of material conditions by combining and appropriately utilizing the power of the mind. Much like applied chemistry creates something new and unique out of careful combinations of chemicals the mastery of mental chemistry...　New Age Pages 354

☐ **The Letters of Robert Browning and Elizabeth Barret Barrett 1845-1846 vol II**　ISBN: *1-59462-193-4*　**$35.95**
by Robert Browning and Elizabeth Barrett　Biographies Pages 596

☐ **Gleanings In Genesis (volume I)** *by Arthur W. Pink*　ISBN: *1-59462-130-6*　**$27.45**
Appropriately has Genesis been termed "the seed plot of the Bible" for in it we have, in germ form, almost all of the great doctrines which are afterwards fully developed in the books of Scripture which follow...　Religion/Inspirational Pages 420

☐ **The Master Key** *by L. W. de Laurence*　ISBN: *1-59462-001-6*　**$30.95**
In no branch of human knowledge has there been a more lively increase of the spirit of research during the past few years than in the study of Psychology, Concentration and Mental Discipline. The requests for authentic lessons in Thought Control, Mental Discipline and...　New Age/Business Pages 422

☐ **The Lesser Key Of Solomon Goetia** *by L. W. de Laurence*　ISBN: *1-59462-092-X*　**$9.95**
This translation of the first book of the "Lemegton" which is now for the first time made accessible to students of Talismanic Magic was done, after careful collation and edition, from numerous Ancient Manuscripts in Hebrew, Latin, and French...　New Age/Occult Pages 92

☐ **Rubaiyat Of Omar Khayyam** *by Edward Fitzgerald*　ISBN:*1-59462-332-5*　**$13.95**
Edward Fitzgerald, whom the world has already learned, in spite of his own efforts to remain within the shadow of anonymity, to look upon as one of the rarest poets of the century, was born at Bredfield, in Suffolk, on the 31st of March, 1809. He was the third son of John Purcell...　Music Pages 172

☐ **Ancient Law** *by Henry Maine*　ISBN: *1-59462-128-4*　**$29.95**
The chief object of the following pages is to indicate some of the earliest ideas of mankind, as they are reflected in Ancient Law, and to point out the relation of those ideas to modern thought.　Religiom/History Pages 452

☐ **Far-Away Stories** *by William J. Locke*　ISBN: *1-59462-129-2*　**$19.45**
"Good wine needs no bush, but a collection of mixed vintages does. And this book is just such a collection. Some of the stories I do not want to remain buried for ever in the museum files of dead magazine-numbers an author's not unpardonable vanity..."　Fiction Pages 272

☐ **Life of David Crockett** *by David Crockett*　ISBN: *1-59462-250-7*　**$27.45**
"Colonel David Crockett was one of the most remarkable men of the times in which he lived. Born in humble life, but gifted with a strong will, an indomitable courage, and unremitting perseverance...　Biographies/New Age Pages 424

☐ **Lip-Reading** *by Edward Nitchie*　ISBN: *1-59462-206-X*　**$25.95**
Edward B. Nitchie, founder of the New York School for the Hard of Hearing, now the Nitchie School of Lip-Reading, Inc, wrote "LIP-READING Principles and Practice". The development and perfecting of this meritorious work on lip-reading was an undertaking...　How-to Pages 400

☐ **A Handbook of Suggestive Therapeutics, Applied Hypnotism, Psychic Science**　ISBN: *1-59462-214-0*　**$24.95**
by Henry Munro　Health/New Age/Health/Self-help Pages 376

☐ **A Doll's House: and Two Other Plays** *by Henrik Ibsen*　ISBN: *1-59462-112-8*　**$19.95**
Henrik Ibsen created this classic when in revolutionary 1848 Rome. Introducing some striking concepts in playwriting for the realist genre, this play has been studied the world over.　Fiction/Classics/Plays 308

☐ **The Light of Asia** *by sir Edwin Arnold*　ISBN: *1-59462-204-3*　**$13.95**
In this poetic masterpiece, Edwin Arnold describes the life and teachings of Buddha. The man who was to become known as Buddha to the world was born as Prince Gautama of India but he rejected the worldly riches and abandoned the reigns of power when...　Religion/History/Biographies Pages 170

☐ **The Complete Works of Guy de Maupassant** *by Guy de Maupassant*　ISBN: *1-59462-157-8*　**$16.95**
"For days and days, nights and nights, I had dreamed of that first kiss which was to consecrate our engagement, and I knew not on what spot I should put my lips..."　Fiction/Classics Pages 240

☐ **The Art of Cross-Examination** *by Francis L. Wellman*　ISBN: *1-59462-309-0*　**$26.95**
Written by a renowned trial lawyer, Wellman imparts his experience and uses case studies to explain how to use psychology to extract desired information through questioning.　How-to/Science/Reference Pages 408

☐ **Answered or Unanswered?** *by Louisa Vaughan*　ISBN: *1-59462-248-5*　**$10.95**
Miracles of Faith in China　Religion Pages 112

☐ **The Edinburgh Lectures on Mental Science (1909)** *by Thomas*　ISBN: *1-59462-008-3*　**$11.95**
This book contains the substance of a course of lectures recently given by the writer in the Queen Street Hall, Edinburgh. Its purpose is to indicate the Natural Principles governing the relation between Mental Action and Material Conditions...　New Age/Psychology Pages 148

☐ **Ayesha** *by H. Rider Haggard*　ISBN: *1-59462-301-5*　**$24.95**
Verily and indeed it is the unexpected that happens! Probably if there was one person upon the earth from whom the Editor of this, and of a certain previous history, did not expect to hear again...　Classics Pages 380

☐ **Ayala's Angel** *by Anthony Trollope*　ISBN: *1-59462-352-X*　**$29.95**
The two girls were both pretty, but Lucy who was twenty-one who supposed to be simple and comparatively unattractive, whereas Ayala was credited, as her Bombwhat romantic name might show, with poetic charm and a taste for romance. Ayala when her father died was nineteen...　Fiction Pages 484

☐ **The American Commonwealth** *by James Bryce*　ISBN: *1-59462-286-8*　**$34.45**
An interpretation of American democratic political theory. It examines political mechanics and society from the perspective of Scotsman James Bryce　Politics Pages 572

☐ **Stories of the Pilgrims** *by Margaret P. Pumphrey*　ISBN: *1-59462-116-0*　**$17.95**
This book explores pilgrims religious oppression in England as well as their escape to Holland and eventual crossing to America on the Mayflower, and their early days in New England...　History Pages 268

QTY

The Fasting Cure *by Sinclair Upton*   ISBN: *1-59462-222-1*   **$13.95**
In the Cosmopolitan Magazine for May, 1910, and in the Contemporary Review (London) for April, 1910, I published an article dealing with my experiences in fasting. I have written a great many magazine articles, but never one which attracted so much attention... New Age/Self Help/Health Pages 164

Hebrew Astrology *by Sepharial*   ISBN: *1-59462-308-2*   **$13.45**
In these days of advanced thinking it is a matter of common observation that we have left many of the old landmarks behind and that we are now pressing forward to greater heights and to a wider horizon than that which represented the mind-content of our progenitors... Astrology Pages 144

Thought Vibration or The Law of Attraction in the Thought World   ISBN: *1-59462-127-6*   **$12.95**
by William Walker Atkinson   *Psychology/Religion Pages 144*

Optimism *by Helen Keller*   ISBN: *1-59462-108-X*   **$15.95**
Helen Keller was blind, deaf, and mute since 19 months old, yet famously learned how to overcome these handicaps, communicate with the world, and spread her lectures promoting optimism. An inspiring read for everyone... Biographies/Inspirational Pages 84

Sara Crewe *by Frances Burnett*   ISBN: *1-59462-360-0*   **$9.45**
In the first place, Miss Minchin lived in London. Her home was a large, dull, tall one, in a large, dull square, where all the houses were alike, and all the sparrows were alike, and where all the door-knockers made the same heavy sound... Childrens/Classic Pages 88

The Autobiography of Benjamin Franklin *by Benjamin Franklin*   ISBN: *1-59462-135-7*   **$24.95**
The Autobiography of Benjamin Franklin has probably been more extensively read than any other American historical work, and no other book of its kind has had such ups and downs of fortune. Franklin lived for many years in England, where he was agent... Biographies/History Pages 332

Name	
Email	
Telephone	
Address	
City, State ZIP	

☐ **Credit Card**   ☐ **Check / Money Order**

Credit Card Number	
Expiration Date	
Signature	

Please Mail to: Book Jungle
PO Box 2226
Champaign, IL 61825
or Fax to: 630-214-0564

ORDERING INFORMATION

web*: www.bookjungle.com*
email*: sales@bookjungle.com*
fax*: 630-214-0564*
mail*: Book Jungle PO Box 2226 Champaign, IL 61825*
or PayPal *to sales@bookjungle.com*

Please contact us for bulk discounts

DIRECT-ORDER TERMS

**20% Discount if You Order
Two or More Books**
Free Domestic Shipping!
Accepted: Master Card, Visa,
Discover, American Express

www.ingramcontent.com/pod-product-compliance
Lightning Source LLC
Chambersburg PA
CBHW080735250626
47170CB00010B/2831